James Gauley

Selections from Standard Authors

For the Benefit of the Prison Inmates

James Gauley

Selections from Standard Authors
For the Benefit of the Prison Inmates

ISBN/EAN: 9783744756624

Printed in Europe, USA, Canada, Australia, Japan

Cover: Foto ©Andreas Hilbeck / pixelio.de

More available books at **www.hansebooks.com**

BENEFIT OF THE PRISON INMATES.

Compiled by JAMES GAULEY,
Moral Instructor State Prison at Folsom.

———

"A man never falls so low but that he may rise, and never rises
so high but that he may fall."

———

SACRAMENTO:
STATE OFFICE : : : J. D. YOUNG, SUPT. STATE PRINTING.
1888.

Presented to the inmates of the State Prison at Folsom, with the Editor's kind regards.

PREFACE.

To the Inmates of the State Prison at Folsom, California:

In view of the limited amount of reading matter in the Prison Library, the idea suggested itself to my mind that a pamphlet containing brief and terse extracts from the writings of a few of the best standard authors, together with a few of my own suggestions, might confer a positive benefit upon the younger, and meet the approbation of the older inmates of the Prison, I compiled the one herewith presented. And with the hope that it will be received by you with all its imperfections, and in the same spirit that prompted its compilation, I remain your sincere friend: and also in the belief that "Our greatest glory is not in never falling, but in rising every time we fall."

CONTENTS.

SELECTIONS.

THE READING HABIT.

[RICHARDSON.]

Were I to pray for a taste, says Sir John Herschell, "which should stand me in stead under every variety of circumstances, and be a source of happiness and cheerfulness to me during life, and a shield against its ills, how everything might go amiss, it would be a taste for reading. Give a man this taste, and the means of gratifying it, and you can hardly fail of making him a happy man: unless, indeed, you put into his hands a most perverse selection of books. You place him in contact with the best society in every period of history, with the wisest, the wittiest, the tenderest, the bravest, and the purest characters who have adorned humanity.

" You make him a denizen of all nations—a contemporary of all ages. The world has been created for him. Nothing can supply the place of books. They are cheering and soothing companions in solitude, and in illness or affliction. The wealth of both continents could not compensate for the good they impart."

Fenelon said: " If all the kingdoms of the empire were laid at my feet in exchange for my books and love of reading, I would spurn them all."

And the historian Gibbon, wrote: "A taste for books is the pleasure and glory of my life. I would not exchange it for the glory of the Indies." Mere acquired knowledge belongs to us only like a wooden leg and a wax nose.

" Knowledge attained by means of thinking, resembles our natural limbs, and is the only kind that really belongs to us. Hence the difference between the thinker and the pedant. The intellectual possession of the independent thinker is like a beautiful picture which stands before us—a living thing, with fitting light and shadow, sustained tones, perfect harmony of color.

"That of the merely learned man may be compared to a pallet covered with bright colors. To *know* one good book well, is better than to know something *about* a hundred good books at second hand."

The ordinary reader is profoundly indifferent about style, and will not take the trouble to understand ideas. He keeps to periodicals or light fiction, which enables the mind to loll in its easy chair (so to speak), and see pass before it a series of pleasing images.

An idea, as Mark Pattison says, is an excitant, comes from mind and calls forth mind; an image is a sedative; and most people, when they take up a book, are seeking a sedative.

WHAT BOOKS TO READ.

[EDITOR.]

In view of the shortness of life, and that "there are twenty-five thousand books published annually," and also that there are one hundred millions in the world—one library in France contains three millions—it is not surprising that I am so often asked by the new beginner, and those beginning to read late in life, "What books ought I read?" I would suggest to the former, and to the latter also, that they will very likely derive the following benefits from reading Sir Walter Scott's works:

Firstly, they will very likely obtain, unwittingly perhaps, such a desire for reading, and reading only the best authors, as to prevent them from reading the coarse, weak, and vulgar trash now flooding the country, and working such widespread demoralization throughout the length and breadth of the land, as to arrest the attention of all those who have the least sympathy with their kind.

In a late issue of the "Philadelphia Ledger and Transcript," the editor of that journal says: "Having taught boys to read, society ought to make every possible effort to guide their reading so that their education shall be of advantage to them. At present it seems as though the chief use made of the little learning some boys acquire in school is in the reading of demoralizing books and 'flash' newspapers, whereby they are incited to become thieves and outlaws, in emulation of the heroes pictured in this pernicious literature. Many cases have been reported of late, and only a few days ago six small boys were arrested in New York for robbing grocery stores. From the proceeds of their robberies they bought vile papers and books which they also read together in an old woodshed, where they also drank beer obtained by barter of their stolen provisions. In other words, they had used the little education obtained in public schools to start a school of their own, wherein they could study to be criminals 'without a master.' These are types of hundreds or thousands. * * * * It is a much simpler matter to guide boys and girls in the right way than it is to forcibly restrain or punish them after they have grown to be men and women, have formed bad habits, and perhaps joined the 'criminal classes.'"

Secondly, by reading "Ivanhoe" the reader will obtain as correct an account of the manners, habits, and customs of the people who lived during the "middle ages" as he would obtain from reading "Froissart's Chronicles," which are merely a bundle of dry facts which Froissart obtained in traveling over Europe, and upon which so many historical novels are founded.

Scott's "Tales of a Grandfather" will also give the reader a very correct history of Scotland, and also a graphic and instructive description of the "Border Wars" between the Scotch and English people. In a word, I would advise the reader to read all of Sir Walter Scott's works, with the exception of his "Life of Napoleon," which he evidently wrote for political effect, as well as for the "canny purpose" of filling his purse and the gratification of his prejudices.

The next author I would recommend to the reader is Charles Dickens; because no one, I imagine, could read Dickens without he, the reader, wishing that he were a better man.

If we estimate greatness by the moral effect produced upon the public mind, it is not too much to say that Dickens was the great moralist of the nineteenth century, as no one man ever did half as much as he in correcting and in abolishing the many flagrant abuses that existed in England during the time in which he wrote. And let me add here that, in reading Dickens, the reader should keep constantly in view that he, Dickens, wrote as he did for the express purpose of calling public attention to those abuses,

and not for the purpose of weaving ingenious plots, like those of
G. P. R. James.

Thirdly, by reason of Dickens' great capacity, and the broad
humanitarian feeling he had for his fellow-man, he has enabled
us, to a very great extent, to "see ourselves as others see us," and
also to see, in the poor and lowly, great and noble traits of character, who could not, to paraphrase Pope, "boast of ancestry
whose ignoble blood had crept through scoundrels ever since the
flood."

A late critic, who claims to have been personally acquainted
with several persons from whom Dickens drew his characters,
says that Dickens' characters are mere "phantoms." While the
critic's statement may be true in a few instances, it cannot be
true in the main, for the reason that we meet with Dickens' characters in every-day life. I am of the opinion that if the critic
referred to would station himself at the corner of Pine and Mont-
gomery Streets, in San Francisco, he would see fifty "Micaw-
bers" within as many minutes "waiting for something to turn
up." And if the critic, before leaving his post, should ask a
"Forty-niner" if he had ever cabined with a "Quilp," or an old
sailor if he had ever had a "Quilp" for a shipmate, that he, the
critic, would receive an affirmative answer in both cases.

And as for "Pecksniffs," they are to be found in every community
wherein "Christian statesmen" thirst for gold "and try to cheat
the devil by joining the church." After having carefully read
Scott and Dickens, I would recommend the reader to read the
"British Essayists;" as the reading of them will cause the reader
to have more expanded views, prevent, to a very great extent, his
mind from running in a groove, and from jumping at the conclusion that God, in His divine wisdom, has not accorded to him, the
reader, any more of His divine inspiration than He has accorded
to the balance of mankind.

Such, at least, are a few of the impressions that the reading of
the "British Essayists" have made upon my mind, and I trust
will make upon yours also. And I would further suggest that,
before commencing to read the history of Rome, or that of any
other foreign country, you not only read the history of your own,
but also make yourself thoroughly acquainted with the funda-
mental laws upon which your country is based, as it is a duty

you owe to yourself and to each and every one of your country-
men.

I will not presume to instruct the average reader in what books
to read, but merely lay before him what a few of the most eminent writers have said upon the subject.

Dr. McCosh says: "The book to read is not the one that thinks
for you, but the one that makes you think." And another author
which I cannot now recall says: "It is the cream of a writer's
thoughts that you want, the kernel and not the shell; the strong,
pungent essence and not the thin, diluted mixture. You should
value a book for its suggestiveness even more than for the information it contains."

Mr. Ruskin says that: "The real value of any book, to a particular reader, is to be measured by its serviceableness to that
reader." And DeQuincey says: "There is a literature of knowledge, and a literature of power, and a knowledge that can never
be transmuted into power becomes mere intellectual rubbish."

The choice of books would be greatly aided, if the reader, in
taking up a volume, would ask himself just why he is going to
read it, and of what service it is going to be to him. This question, if sincerely put, and truthfully answered, is pretty sure to
lead him to the great books—or at least to the books that are
great for him. Homer, Plutarch, Herodotus, and Plato; Virgil,
Livy, and Tacitus; Dante, Tasso, and Petrarch; Cervantes;
Thomas á Kempis; Goethe and Schiller; Chaucer, Spencer,
Shakespeare, Milton, Bacon, Sir Thomas Brown, Bunyan, Addi-
son, Gray, Scott, Wordsworth, and Hawthorne—he who reads
these, and such as these, is not in serious danger of spending his
time amiss.

But not even such a list as this is to be received as a necessity
by every reader. One may find Cowper more profitable than
Wordsworth; to another, the reading of Bancroft may be more
advantageous than that of Herodotus; while a third may gain
more immediate and lasting good from great historical novels
like Eber's "Wavada," or Kingsley's "Hypatia," than from a long
and patient attempt to master Grote's "History of Greece," or
Gibbon's "Decline and Fall of the Roman Empire." Each individual reader must try, first of all, what is the best for himself.

In forming this decision let him make the utmost use of the

best guide, not forgetting that the average opinion of educated men is pretty sure to be a correct opinion; but never let him put aside his own honesty and individuality. He must choose his books as he chooses his friends, because of their integrity and helpfulness, and because of the pleasure their society gives him. " Every book that we take up without a purpose," says Mr. Frederick Harrison, " is an opportunity lost of taking up a book with a purpose." Every bit of stray information that we cram into our heads without any sense of its importance, is for the most part a bit of the most useful information driven out of our heads and choked off from our minds.

It is so certain that information, that is, the knowledge, the stored thoughts and observations of mankind, are now grown to proportions so utterly incalculable and prodigious, that even the learned, whose lives are given to study, can only pick up some crumbs that fall from the table of truth.

They delve and tend but a plot in that vast and teeming kingdom, whilst those whom active life leaves with but a few cramped hours of study can hardly come to know the very vastness of the field before them, or how infinitesimally is the corner they can traverse at the best.

We know all is not of equal value. We know that books differ in value as much as diamonds differ from the sand on the sea-shore, as much as our living friend differs from a dead rat. We know that in the myriad-peopled world of books very much in all kinds is trivial, enervating, inane, even noxious. And thus, where we have infinite opportunities of wasting our efforts to the end of satisfying our minds without enriching them, of clogging the spirit without satisfying it, there I cannot but think the very infinity of opportunities is robbing us of the actual power of using them. And thus I come often, in my less hopeful moods, to watch the remorseless cataract of daily literature which thunders over the remnants of the past, as if it were a fresh impediment to the men of our day in the way of systematic knowledge and consistent powers of thought, as if it were destined one day to overwhelm the great inheritance of mankind in prose and verse.

I am not presumptuous enough to assert that the large part of modern literature is not worth reading in itself, that the large part of modern literature is not readable, entertaining, one may say, highly instructive.

Nor do I pretend that the verses which we read so zealously in place of Milton's are not good verses. On the contrary, I think them sweetly conceived, as musical and as graceful as the verse of any age in our history. I say it emphatically, a great deal of our modern literature is such that it is exceedingly difficult to resist it and undeniable that it gives us real information.

It seems perhaps unreasonable to many to assert that a decent, readable book which gives us actual instruction can be otherwise than a useful companion and solid gain.

I do say many people are ready to cry out upon me as an obstructionist for venturing to doubt a general confidence in all literature, simply as such. But the question which weighs upon me with such crushing force is this: What are the books in our little remnant of reading time it is most vital for us to know?

For the true use of books is of such sacred value to us that to be simply entertained is to cease to be taught, elevated, inspired by books; merely to gather information of a chance kind is to close the mind to knowledge of the urgent kind.

This union of freedom with authority—of a choice for one's self, and a willingness to believe that the world is right in setting Shakespeare above Swinburne, and Homer above Tupper is, I believe, the true and the only guide in the selection of books to read. In the long run, nothing but truth, simplicity, purity, and a lofty purpose approves a book to the favor of the ages; and nothing else ought to approve it to the individual reader.

Thus the end is reached and the choice is made, not by taking a book because a "course of reading commands you to do so, but because you come to see for yourself the wisdom of the selection. The pure and wholesome heart of humanity—that thing which we call conscience—is the guide of readers as it is of every other class of works in life."

Mr. Harrison in another place says: "I have no intention to moralize or to indulge in a homily against the reading of what is deliberately evil. There is not so much need for this now, and I am not discoursing on the whole duty of man. I take that part of our reading which is by itself, no doubt, harmless, entertaining, and even gently instructive.

" But of this enormous mass of literature how much deserves to be chosen out, to be preferred to all the great books of the world, to be set apart for those precious hours which are all that the most of us can give to solid reading? The vast proportion of books, are books that we should never be able to read.

"A serious percentage of books are not worth reading at all. The really vital books we also know to be a very trifling portion of the whole. And yet we act as if every book were as good as any other, as if it were merely a question of order which we take up first, as if any book were good enough for us, and as if all were alike honorable, precious, and satisfying.

" Alas! books can not be more than the men who write them, and as a large proportion of the human race now write books, with motives and objects as various as human activity, books, as books are entitled, *a priori*, until their value is proved to the same attention and respect as houses, steam engines, pictures, fiddles, bonnets, and other thoughtful or ornamental products of human industry."

"The Bible," Emerson says, "has been the literature as well as the religion of all large portions of Europe—Havis was the eminent genius of the Persians, Confucius of the Chinese, Cervantes of the Spaniards. With this pilot of genius, let the student read one, or let him read many, he will read advantageously."

POETRY.

[RICHARDSON.]

Some people read a great deal of poetry with constant zest and unfailing advantage; others, though they may be " great readers " of other classes of literature, find little pleasure or profit in poetry. Is it a duty to read poetry? Should those who seem to have no natural taste for it, endeavor to cultivate a taste; or should they rest content with the conclusion that some minds have no capacity for its enjoyment?

It may not be a downright duty to like poetry, or to try to like it; but certainly it is a misfortune that so large and lovely a division of the world's literature should be lost to any reader. The absence of a poetic taste is a sad indication of a lack of the imaginative faculty, and without imagination what is life.

The study and reading of poetry, says President Porter, "exercises and cultivates the imagination, and in this way imparts intellectual power. It is impossible to read the products of any poet's imagination without using our own. To read what he creates is to recreate in our own minds the images and pictures which first conceived and then expressed in language."

If a reader finds that the ideal has little or no place in his intellectual life, or in his daily process of thought and feeling, then he should consider, with all soberness, the fact that a God-giving power is slipping away from him—a power without which his best faculties must become atrophied; without which he loses the greater half of the enjoyment of life. day by day; without which, in very truth, he cannot see all the glory of the open door of the Kingdom of Heaven.

Children are poets; they see fairy-land in a poor, broken set of toy crockery, or in a ragged company of broken-nosed dolls. Their powers of imagination ought never to be lost in the humdrum affairs of a work-a-day world; their habit of finding the real in the ideal is one which cannot be laid aside without great detriment to the individual life and character.

There may then be persons who "have no capacity for poetry," and who cannot cultivate a taste for it: but this inability, if real, is to be mourned as a mental blindness and deafness, shutting out whole worlds from sight and hearing. There is, of course, a great deal of imaginative literature which is not poetry, in the technical sense: but if one can read Hawthorne or Richter with pleasure, he is quite sure to find no stumbling-block in Schiller's "Lay of the Bell," or Drake's "Culprit Fay."

It is the poetic spirit that we should recognize and take to our hearts, whatever be the outward form in which it may be enshrined.

What is the poetic spirit? Many have been the attempts to define it; but, after all, we can only say, in the words Shelley wrote in his "Hymn to the Spirit of Nauve," "all feel, yet see thee never." Or again, is not poetry to be described, as nearly as we may describe it, in two more lines from the same poem: .

Lamp of earth where'er thou movest,
Its dim shapes are clad with brightness.

In Professor W. P. Atkinson's lecture on reading, is a passage concerning poetry, which is both imaginative and practical. "I have no thought," says he, "of attempting here a definition of poetry, though I should like to come and give you a lecture on the art of reading it."

Whether we call it, with Aristotle, imitation; whether we say more worthily, with Bacon, that it was even thought to have some participation of divineness, because it doth raise and erect the mind by submitting the shows of things to the desires of the mind; whereas reason doth buckle and bow the mind unto the nature of things; whether in modern times we define it, with Shelley, as " the best and happiest thoughts of the best and happiest minds;" or say, with Matthew Arnold, that "poetry is simply the most beautiful, impressive, and widely effective mode of saying things;" and again, that "it is to the poetical literature of an age that we must in general look for the most perfect and most adequate interpretation of that age;" or, whether we say, with the greatest poet of the làst generation, that "poetry is the breath and finer spirit of all knowledge, the impassioned expression which is in the countenance of all science"—all I am concerned to say here is that poetry is that branch of the literature of power preëminently worthy of study, and that without study we shall know but little about it. We need not think, then, that the reading of poetry is a matter of whim or accident to be undertaken without thought or study. President Porter says that a "taste for poetry, especially that of the higher order, is to a great extent the product of special culture." The foundation for this culture lies in the individual mind; for its development he must seek his material from the treasures around him, and must work out his methods of utilizing that material with the same care, or even greater, which he applies to other departments of intellectual exercise.

Let him, if he finds his taste in need of cultivation, begin with such poems as he likes; read them more than once; learn their teachings; apprehend their inner spirit and purpose. Whatever the beginning, it is sure to lead to something better, if the reader will but resolutely determine to know what the writer meant to say; to see the picture that he portrayed; and to share his enthusiasm and warmth of feeling. Mr. G. F. Goshen, a leading English banker and political economist, declares that the cultivation of the imagination is essential to the highest success in politics, in learning, and in the commercial business of life. No one is too dull, too prosaic, or too much absorbed in the routine of "practical life" to be absolved from the care of his imaginative powers, and no one is likely to find that this care will not repay him, even in a practical sense. He who thinks wisely, he who perceives quickly that which others do not see at all, is better equipped for any work than one whose mind works slowly and feebly, and whose apprehensions have grown rusty from disease. Poetry is not for the few, but for the many, for all. The world's great poems, absolutely without exception, have been poems whose meaning has been perfectly clear and whose language has been simple—poems which have addressed themselves to the plain and common sense of the ages.

Obscurity and whimsicality may belong to the Brownings of literature, to the star-gazing Transcendentalists of 1840, or to the posturing impressionists of to-day, but Homer, and Virgil, and Dante, and Chaucer, and Shakespeare need no mystical commentary to explain their meaning; like Mark Antony, they "only speak right on."

If a poem is obscure, you may know by that mark alone that it is a second-rate or tenth-rate affair, and that it is not worth your while to vex your brain over it at all. If a poet has not made himself clear, it is his fault and not yours, if you are a person of average intellectual capacity. Feel not abashed if you do not comprehend the "orphil" or the "intense;" most likely the author did not comprehend it himself.

Sunlight, air. water—these are not for the few; nor is poetry to be cooped and confined any more than these.

Principal Sharp thus speaks of this inherent quality of the best poetry—a quality which all men may apprehend if they will: "The pure style is that which, whether it describes a scene, a character, or a sentiment, lays hold of its inner meaning, not its surface; the type which the thing embodies, not the accidents; the core or heart of it, not the accessories. * * * Descriptions of this kind, while they convey typical conceptions, yet retain perfect individuality. They are done by a few strokes, in the fewest possible words; but each stroke tells, each word goes home.

Of this kind is the poetry of the psalms and of the Hebrew prophets. It is seen in the brief impressive way in which Dante presents the heroes or heroines of his nether world, as compared with Virgil's more elaborate pictures. In all of Wordsworth that has really impressed the world, this will be found to be the chief characteristic. It is seen especially in his finest lyrics and his most impressive sonnets. Take only three poems that stand together in his works—"Glen Almain," "Stepping Westward," the "Solitary Reaper"—in each you have a scene and its sentiment brought home with the minimum of words, the maximum of power. It is distinctive of the pure style that it relies not on side effect, but on the total impression, that it produces a unity in which all the parts are subordinated to one paramount aim. The imagery is appropriate, never excessive. You are not distracted by glaring single lines or too splendid images. There is one tone, and that all pervading, reducing all the materials, however diverse, into harmony with the one total result designed.

"This style, in its perfection, is not to be obtained by any rules of art. The secret of it lies further in than rules of art can reach, even in this: that the writer sees his object, and this only; feels the sentiment of it, and this only; is so absorbed in it, lost in it, that he altogether forgets himself and his style, and cares only in fewest, most vital words, to convey to others the vision his own soul sees. *   *   *   *   *   *   *   *   *

"The ornate style of poetry is altogether different from this. No doubt the multitude of uneducated and half educated readers which every day increases, loves a highly ornamented, not to say a meretricious style, both in literature and in the arts; and if these demand it, writers and artists will be found to furnish it. There remains, therefore, to the most educated, the task of counter-working this evil. With them it lies to elevate the thought and to purify the taste of less cultivated readers, and so to remedy one of the evils incident to democracy. To high thinking, and noble living, the pure style is natural. But these things are severe, require moral bracing, minds not luxurious but which can endure hardness. Softness, self pleasing and moral limpness, find their congenial element in excess of highly-colored ornamentation. On the whole, when once a man is master of himself and of his materials, the best rule that can be given him is to forget style altogether, and to think only of the reality to be expressed. "The more the mind is intent on the reality, the simpler, truer, more telling the style will be. The advice which the great preacher gives for conduct holds not less for all kinds of writing. Aim at things, and your words will be right without aiming. Guard against love of display, love of singularity, love of seeming original. Aim at meaning what you say, and saying what you mean.

"When a man is full of his subject and has matured his powers of expression, sets himself to speak thus simply and sincerely, whatever there is in him of strength or sweetness, of dignity or grace, of humor or pathos, will find its way out naturally into his language. That language will be true to his thoughts, true to the man himself."

How different is such poetical language from the poetry of the obscure, or the mock sentimental, or the positively base! What the "Saturday Review" has said of Byron is true of many another poet: "Even Byron's best passages will not stand critical examination. They excite rather than transport, and when the reader examines seriously what he has felt, the impression of a vague, contagious excitement is all that he retains. In reading Byron, the reader dimly feels that he is in the presence of a very eloquent person, who is, or would like to be thought, in a state of excitement about something, and that it is his duty to become excited too." True poetry has a far nobler mission than to puzzle, or to amuse, or to excite; it is the voice of all that is best in humanity, speaking from man to man. Not all of us can thus speak, but we can all hear, and incorporate what we hear in our best and truest life, day by day.

2

THOUGHTS FOR A YOUNG MAN.

[HORACE MANN.]

The pleasure of literature may rightfully accept a portion of the time not demanded by business or by health. The pursuits of science are even more valuable and ennobling than the study of literature. Literature is mainly conversant with the work of man, while science deals with the works of God; and the difference in the subject-matter of the two indicates the difference in their relative value, and in the power and happiness they can respectively bestow. A great portion of our literature is addressed to marvelousness, ideality, and those subordinate faculties that are brought into play by narrative adventure, and scenic representation.

By far the larger part of all histories, a great portion of epic poetry, and almost all martial poetry are addressed to the loutish propensities of combativeness and destructiveness. But physical science addresses itself to the noble faculty of causality and the kindred members of its groups, including the mathematical powers; and ethical science addresses itself both to causality and to conscientiousness, and seeks also the sacred sanctions of veneration for whatever it teaches.

A vast proportion of our literature consists of what had been written before the truths of modern science were discovered: before the idea that there is an order of nature, and a law of cause and effect, in the spiritual as well as in the natural world, had been received into the mind, and had modified its action; and nothing can be more different than what the same genius would write before being imbued with the spirit of science, and after being so imbued.

All science may be invested with the charms of literature, but in such cases it does not cease to be science; it only becomes science beautified.

Hence the poet or the moralist *may be scientific* men, though they rarely have been.

Before the time of Lord Bacon, men invented laws for nature, instead of inquiring of nature by what laws she wrought. Since his time, men have condescended to interrogate nature instead of dictating to her; and already we have a physical world as different from that known before he wrote, as we can imagine any two plants to be from each other.

A vast proportion of the existing literature has as little relation to metaphysical truth, as the speculations of the schoolmen, before the time of Bacon, had to physical laws.

It is not more true that Aristotle and his followers invented laws for nature which she never owned, and explained her phenomena on principles that never existed, than it is that most of those works, which we call works of the imagination, assume the existence of spiritual laws, such spiritual laws as the spirit of man never knew, and therefore produce results of action and character such as all experience repudiates. Hence it is, that I would commend science more than literature as an improver of the mind.

Such a state of things needs not to be, and probably ere long will cease to be. Gall, Spurzheim, and Combe, have done much for physics, or the laws of matter. Already their labors are entirely appreciated: they are producing great improvements and ameliorations in penal jurisprudence and prison discipline, in the treatment of the insane, in ethical philosophy, and in education, which lies at the bottom of all subjects, which, as it seems to me, can never be properly understood but in the light of their science.

A WORD TO THE YOUNGER INMATES OF THE PRISON.

[EDITOR.]

As soon as you have learned to read a paragraph in a newspaper, without stopping to spell every word contained in it, do not jump at the conclusion that you will be taken for a philosopher by propounding questions which you have accidentally stumbled upon in glancing over the pages of Voltaire, Volney, Hume, Thomas Paine, or any other infidel writer. Because if you do you will very likely be forced into a position that will cause you to expose the extent of your ignorance, to say nothing of your consummate impudence, in presuming to propound questions that have taxed the greatest minds that the world has ever seen.

Hume, the historian, taxed his mind for seven years with the proposition, "Whether mind created matter, or whether matter and mind were coexistent," and then at the expiration of the seven years went crazy. So you see how idle, and worse than idle, it would be for an uncultivated mind like your own to waste your time in propounding, parrot-like, the few "smart" questions which a great mind like that of Hume failed to solve.

THE ART OF SKIPPING.

[RICHARDSON.]

It is a fortunate thing that one of the most hackneyed quotations concerning books and reading should also be one of the most sensible ones—Lord Bacon's saying, that "some books are to be tasted, others to be swallowed, and some few to be chewed and digested; that is, some books are to be read only in part, others to be read, but not curiously, and some few to be read wholly, and with diligence and attention."

The following of this piece of advice has done a great deal of good, and no harm is likely to come from its wise observance. Some people profess to believe that a book that is worth reading at all is worth reading straight through; a piece of foolishness that would be paralleled by an insistance upon eating a tableful every time one sits down to a meal. A person who makes up his mind to read all of a book or none must be fully convinced of the solemn truth of the saying that "a book's a book, although there is nothing in 't." Against such lack of wisdom the sturdy common sense of Lord Bacon's remark may be put. The reader need but rest assured of its unquestionable truth and spend his time in trying to discover what books are to be tasted, what swallowed, and what digested, rather than vex his soul in questioning whether the general advice is sound or not.

A book that is worth reading all through is pretty sure to make its worth known. There is something in the literary conscience which tells a reader whether he is wasting his time or not. An hour, a minute, may be sufficient opportunity for forming a decision concerning the worth or worthlessness of the book.

If it is utterly bad and valueless then skip the whole of it as soon as you have made the discovery. If a part is good and a part bad, accept the one and reject the other. If you are in doubt, take warning at the first intimation that you are misspending your opportunity and frittering away your time over an unprofitable book. Reading that is of questionable value is not hard to find out; it bears its notes and marks in unmistakable plainness, and it puts forth, all unwittingly, danger signals, of which the reader should take heed.

The art of skipping is, in a word, the art of noting and shunning that which is bad, or frivolous, or misleading, or unsuitable for one's individual needs. If you are convinced that the book or the chapter is bad, you cannot drop it too quickly. If it is simply idle and foolish, put it away on that account, unless you are properly seeking amusement from idleness and frivolity. If it is deceitful and disingenuous, your task is not so easy; but your conscience will give you warning, and the sharp examination which should follow will tell you that you are in poor literary company. But there are a great many books which are good in themselves, and yet are not good at all times or for all readers. No book, indeed, is of universal value and appropriateness. The individual must always dare to remember that he has his own legitimate tastes and wants, and that it is not only proper to follow them, but highly improper to permit them to be overruled by the tastes and wants of others. It is right for one to neglect entirely, or to skip through, pages which another should study again and again.

Let each reader ask himself: Why am I reading this? what service will it be to me? am I neglecting something else that would be more profitable? Hence, as in every other question involved in the choice of books, the golden key to knowledge, a key that will only fit its own proper doors, is *purpose*. Thus the reader is the pupil, and the companion, and the fellow-worker of the author, not his slave.

"It is a wise book that is good from title page to the end," says A. Bronson Alcott. Such a book should be read through; but the books that are wise in spots should be read in spots.

Again, Mr. Alcott says: "I value books for their suggestiveness even more than for the information they contain; volumes that may be taken in hand and laid aside, read at odd moments, containing sentences that take possession of my thought and prompt to the following them into their wider relations with life and things." This suggestiveness of books read at odd moments is one of the great advantages of judicious skipping. From this habit comes, often, a riper and wholesomer harvest than would spring from the most painstaking devotion to regulated and routine reading and study.

One page, one sentence, thus planted in the fertile soil of a receptive mind, is better than a whole library read from a mere sense of duty, and without reference to one's true welfare, as indicated by his nature and his needs. No one thus wisely choosing what he may best read, need be in any fear that he is a superficial reader. "Did you ever happen to see," asks a writer whose name I have unfortunately lost, "did you ever happen to see, in shrewd, old hard-headed Bishop Whately's annotations on Lord Bacon's essays, a good passage about what is and what is not superficiality? It is in the sentence in Bacon's essays, on studies, 'Crafty men contemn studies.' This 'contempt,' says the Bishop, whether of crafty men or narrow-minded men, finds its expression in the word 'smattering,' and the couplet is become almost a proverb:

A little learning is a dangerous thing;
Drink deep, or taste not the Pierian spring."

But the poet's remedies for the dangers of a little learning are both of them impossible. No one can drink deep enough to be in truth anything more than superficial; and every human being that is not a downright idiot must taste.

And the Bishop, in his downright way, goes on to give practical illustrations of the usefulness of a little knowledge, and proceeds: "What, then, is the smattering, the imperfect and superficial knowledge that deserve contempt?

"A slight and superficial knowledge is justly condemned when it is put in the place of more full and exact knowledge.

"Such an acquaintance with chemistry and anatomy, for instance, as would be creditable and not useless to a lawyer, would be contemptible for a physician; and such acquaintance with law as would be desirable for him, would be a most discreditable smattering for a lawyer."

Mr. Hamerton has some wise words on this subject: "It becomes a necessary part," says he, "of the art of intellectual living, so to order our work as to shield ourselves if possible, at least during a certain portion of our time, from the evil consequences of hurry. The whole secret lies in a single word—selection. * * * The art is to select the reading which will be most useful to our purpose, and, in writing, to select the words which will express our meaning with the greatest clearness in a little space.

"The art of reading is to skip judiciously. Whole libraries may be skipped in these days, when we have the results of them in our modern culture without going over the ground again. And even the books we decide to read there are almost always large portions which do not concern us, and which we are sure to forget the day after we have read them."

The art is to skip all that does not concern us, whilst missing nothing that we really need. No external guidance can teach us this; for nobody but ourselves can guess what the needs of our intellects may be.

But let us select with decisive firmness, independently of other people's advice, independently of the authority of custom. Of course it follows that to some extent we can let others do the work of selecting for us, subject to correction whenever necessary. " In comparing the number of good books with the shortness of life, many might well be read by proxy, if we had good proxies," says Emerson.

Sensible literary guides must be followed to a large extent, whether in their recommendation of one book as against another, or of certain poems or prose extracts in comparison with others.

Books of selection, it is true, sometimes omit things we would have greatly liked; but who will pretend to say that he always finds everything that would have pleased or profited him, even when he makes his own choice?

As no worker in any field of labor can, in this social world, dispense with the help of others, so it is especially necessary for readers to follow the guidance of pioneers and wise critics, and to make use of the selections these critics have made, as well as their indication of whole books. And sometimes, as Emerson's remark shows us, we may not only delegate to others the work of choice and selection, but also that of reading itself.

REMEMBERING WHAT ONE READS.

[RICHARDSON.]

Scarcely anything more annoys readers than the fact that they forget so much of what they have read.

In history, dates and names pass from mind; poems that they once knew by heart fade away from recollection; and the characters, the plots, or perhaps the very titles of stories which were once familiar, depart as utterly as though they had never been known at all.

In connection with this question of the retention or nonretention of what one reads, it should never be forgotten that God has evidently arranged the powers of the human mind in such a way that we *must* forget a great deal, however carefully we strive to remember all we can. A large part of our knowledge, too, is to be considered as nutriment, or as intelligent exercise; and we should no more lament over its loss than because we do not remember what we had for breakfast a year ago to-day, or the exact length of the invigorating walk we took on that breezy morning, week before last.

A book is by no means read without profit, if a part, or even the whole of it, be forgotten beyond recall. And it is a consolation to reflect that the very best use to which some of our past reading can be put, is to be forgotten as speedily as possible. If we have forgotten some things that were good and pleasant, we have luckily blotted from our minds not a little that was noxious and unattractive.

But a "poor memory" is a thing that can be materially strengthened; and after all reservations have been made, we should not forget the duty of remembering all we really ought to remember, so far as the natural powers of our minds will permit. The first and the last aid to memory is a habit of paying strict attention to what we read. "Special efforts should be made to *retain* what is gathered from reading," says President Porter, "if any such efforts are required. Some persons read with an interest so wakeful and responsive, and an attention so fixed and energetic, as to need no appliance and no efforts in order to retain what they read. They look upon a page and it is imprinted upon the memory. * * *

" But there are others who read only to lose and to forget.

" Facts and truths, words and thoughts, are alike evanescent.

" We shall not attempt to explain here the nature of these differences. We are concerned only to devise the remedy; we insist that those who labor under these difficulties should use special appliances to avoid or overcome them.

" But that upon which we insist most of all, is that what we read we should seek to make our own, only in the manner and after the measure of which we are capable."

President Porter then goes on to advise each reader to follow his natural bent and aptitudes; not to worry if he has not a good verbal memory, over his inability to remember choice phrases or striking stanzas, nor to vex his soul over his failure to retain names and dates. " When a man reads," he says. " he should put himself into the most intimate intercourse with his author, so that all his energies of apprehension, judgment, and feeling may be occupied with, and aroused by, what his author furnishes, whatever it may be. If repetition or review will aid him in this, as it often will, let him not disdain or neglect frequent reviews. If the use of the pen in brief or full notes, in catch words or symbols, will aid him, let him not shrink from the drudgery of the pen and the common-place book."

Philip Gilbert Hamerton has expressed an opinion that what is called a "defective memory," is by no means an unmixed evil.

He says there is such a thing as a "selecting memory, which is not only useful for what it retains, but for what it rejects.

" What really *interests* us, we can usually retain without recourse to any elaborate system of memories.

" That which does not properly interest us we cannot thus retain. Bad memories are often the best selecting memories.

" They seldom win distinction in examinations; but in literature and art they are quite incomparably superior to the miscellaneous memories that receive only as boxes and drawers receive what is put into them.

" A good literary or artistic memory is not like a Post Office that takes in everything, but like a very well edited periodical, which prints nothing that does not harmonize with its intellectual life."

CONVERSATION.

Professor Matthews says: "Fox acknowledged that he had derived more political information from Burke's conversation alone than from books, sciences, and all his worldly experience put together." The same author further says: Conversation is as necessary as meditation to the highest culture. And what is more delightful than this communion of thinkers? Pleasant it is to sit in a library or study, with a goodly array of wise or charming books about you, in which are preserved, as in a vial, the precious "life blood" of the world's master spirits; or, with the choicest of those "abstracts and brief chronicles of the times," the newspapers, to tell how flows the warm life-blood of the world, and how the car of progress goes thundering along the high roads.

Pleasant is it, with paper-knife in hand, to skim the contents of the last monthly magazines brimming with the freshest wit and wisdom of the day; but pleasanter far than any of these is communion with living men whose conversation is full of "that seasoned life of men which is stored up in books," who have roamed through all the fields of literature, and gathering the choicest flowers have arranged them for your delight. Reading is a great pleasure, but it is solitary. Byron says:

They who true joy would win
Must share it; happiness is born twin.

True as this generally is it is doubly true of literary enjoyment. The fullest instruction and the fullest enjoyment are never derived from books till we have ventilated the ideas thus obtained in free and easy chat with others.

The mental faculties demand exercise as truly as the bodily, and enjoy it as keenly. The mind that is healthy delights in the glow of movement and contest.

It loves to meet with a congenial spirit—one that has sucked the sweetness of the same authors, and enjoyed them with the same gust—which has brought away their quaint essence, and treats it to the juice of the grape without thrusting upon it the stalks and husks.

Talking is a digestive process which is absolutely essential to the mental construction of the man who devours many books. A full mind must have talk, or it will grow dyspeptic.

Sir William Hamilton used to say that a man never knows anything until he has taught it in some way; it may be orally, or it may be in writing a book. It is equally true that many authors have talked better than they have written. Philosophers tell us that knowledge is precious for its own sake; that it is its own exceeding great reward. But experience tells us that knowledge is not knowledge until the use of it; that it is not ours until we have brought it under the dominion of the great social faculty—speech. Solitary reading will enable a man to stuff himself with information; but without conversation his mind will become like a pond without an outlet—a mass of unhealthy stagnature.

It is not enough to harvest knowledge by study; the wind of talk must winnow it, and blow away the chaff; then will the clear, bright grains of wisdom be garnered for our own use or that of others.

Then let us talk; and that our talk may be a true recreation, let us talk with congenial spirits. Such spirits may be met with singly in the ordinary intercourse of life, but the full play of the mind demands that they should be encountered, "not in single spies, but in battalions;" and hence the necessity of clubs to bring together, like steel filings out of sand at the approach of a magnet, men of the most opposite pursuits and tastes, the attrition of whose minds may brush away their rust and cobwebs, and give them edge and polish.

Henry Giles says: Nothing is better than conversation as a corrective of self-sufficiency. In educated conversation a man soon finds his level. He learns more truly than from books, in converse with living men, to estimate his powers modestly and justly. A book is passive; it does not repel pretention; it does not rebuke vanity. Indeed, reading and study become to many but the nurture of conceit. If some persons value themselves on the books they own, it is not surprising that others should value themselves on the books they read. As knowledge grows on the thoughts in books, so pedantry feeds on their words, and is proud, poor, lean, and solitary. In conversation a man is not long in discovering that he alone does not know everything, and that though *he* were to die, wisdom would not perish with him. In conversation, intelligent men, comparing themselves among themselves, exercise mutually a silent but a faithful criticism, which, thought just and candid, is not indulgent; which, though not indulgent, is not ungenerous: and which does as much to cement a brotherly companionship as it ministers to mutual improvement. Conversation, while correcting the mind, enlarges it. We share in the fruits of other minds, and of minds more productive than our own.

The power that comes to us from without, strengthens the power that is within. A man's thought is original by the peculiarity of his mental constitution; so far as he has a thought at all, it must, in some sense, be a thought distinct from every other man's thought. It is shaped in the mould of his individual intellect; it is colored by the atmosphere of his emotional and moral character. A man's thought is shaped by the peculiarity of his personal history, mental and otherwise. He has thus an experience, memories, feelings, and associations through which none but himself have gone. All these are more or less involved in any word that a man can truly bring out of himself, any word that is the transcript of a soul-grown idea. The most honest man, the most simple-minded man, will often fail of this distinctive utterance in methodical composition and set speech.

The individuality of his idea, of his being, are diluted into verbiage, or they become lost in the misty haze of commonplace. Conversation permits him to wait for the right word, and supplies the unbidden inspiration that can speak it rightly. Thus you gather in from every side the realities of mind; the realities of life.

The poorest leaves with you something which might have been loss not to have acquired. This and all such acquirements enter into experience. Experience consists of feelings and knowledge transmuted into life. Memory and observation gather in the materials; imagination and reflection work the transformation. Every region of apprehensible existence supplies materials, but in nothing as in human character are materials of such value; and in conversation, human character most undesignedly reveals itself. Other men studied from our own position; ourselves studied from theirs; the world contemplated alternately from both; these, I take it, are the elements of experience; and in conversation we have them all combined.

BOOK KNOWLEDGE.

[CHESTERFIELD.]

I have this evening been tired, jaded, nay, tormented, by the company of a most worthy, sensible, and learned man—a near relation of mine—who dined and passed the evening with me. This seems a paradox, but is a plain truth; he has no knowledge of the world, no manners, no address; far from talking without book, as is commonly said of people who talk silly, he only talks by book; which in general conversation is ten times worse. He has formed in his own closet, from books, certain systems of everything, argues tenaciously upon those principles, and is both surprised and angry at whatever deviates from them. His theories are good, but unfortunately are impracticable. Why? Because he has only read, and not conversed.

LEARN TO BE BRIEF.

[EDITOR.]

Long visits, long stories, long exhortations, and long prayers, seldom profit those who have to do with them. Life is short, time is short. Moments are precious. Learn to condense, abridge, and intensify. We can endure many an ache and ill, if soon over, while even pleasures grow insipid and intolerable, if they are protracted beyond the limits of reason and convenience.

Learn to be brief; lop off branches; stick to the main fact in your case. If you pray, ask for what you would receive and get through; if you speak, tell your message, and hold your tongue; boil down two words into one, and three into two. "Learn to be brief." Take a lesson from the Lord's Prayer, which is brevity itself.

BREVITIES.

The writers against religion, whilst they oppose every system, are wisely careful never to set up any of their own.—*Edmund Burke.*

Good fortune. like misfortune, comes oftentimes when we least expect it. Consequently we should never jump at the conclusion that we are never to see another happy day.—*Ed.*

As time is money, and money is power, it is evidently the height of folly for a poor man to spend either a cent, or one minute's time, foolishly.

It is one of two things with us in this world. We must be "boss," or else be "bossed."—*Ed.*

However virtuous and exemplary a young man may have been, he is yet within peril of falling; and however vicious and abandoned he may have been, he is yet within hope of saving.—*Horace Mann.*

"The chief misfortunes that befall us in life can be traced to some vices or follies which we have committed."

"They who have nothing to give, can afford relief to others by imparting what they feel."

The temperate are the most truly luxurious. By abstaining from most things, it is surprising how many things we enjoy.—*Samuel Sims.*

"He who lays his hand upon a woman save in the way of kindness, it were base flattery to call him coward."

Query—In denying that we are to be held accountable in the next world for the misdeeds committed in this, is the "wish father to the thought?"—*Ed.*

"Deceit is not sagacity."

"Nothing astonishes men so much as common sense."

"Disappointment and distress are often blessings in disguise."

"In drinking the health of others be careful you do not lose your own."

Lacondaire says: "You cannot imprison reason, you cannot burn up facts, you cannot dishonor virtue, you cannot assassinate logic."

"Most people's ideas are adopted children; few brains can raise a family of their own."

"Luxury, pride, and vanity have frequently as much influence in corrupting the sentiments of the great, as ignorance, bigotry, and prejudice have in misleading the opinions of the multitude."

Luxuries long indulged in become necessities; consequently the poor should never indulge in them for any considerable length of time, as the indulgence is sure to cause more pain than pleasure. The whisky and opium habits, for example.—*Ed.*

GOOD SENSE.
[LORD LYTTON.]

Good sense is not merely intellectual attribute. It is the result of a just equilibrium of all our faculties, spiritual and moral.

The dishonest are the toys of their own passions; may have genius; but they rarely, if ever, have good sense in the conduct of life. They may often win large prizes, but it is a game of chance, not skill. But the man whom I perceive walking an honorable and upright career, just to others and also to himself, is a more dignified representative of his Maker than the mere child of genius. Of such a man, we say, he has good sense; yes, but he has also integrity, self-respect, and self-denial. A thousand trials which his sense braves and conquers are temptations also to his probity, his temper; in a word, to all the many sides of his complicated nature. Now I do not think he will have this good sense any more than a drunkard will have strong nerves, unless he be in the constant habit of keeping his mind clear from the intoxication of envy, vanity, and the various emotions that dupe and mislead us. Good sense is not, therefore, an abstract quality or a solitary talent; it is the natural result of the habit of *thinking justly*, and, therefore, seeing clearly, and is as different from the sagacity that belongs to a diplomatist or an attorney as the philosophy of Socrates differs from the rhetoric of Georgias.

LEARN HOW TO REASON.

[EDITOR.]

The great distinguishing feature between man and brute being reason, it is astonishing that the poorer portion of mankind who cannot afford to make a mistake or to commit an error. do not give this subject more thought.

Particularly when we take into consideration that their manhood, their liberty, and their very lives, oftentimes depend upon a judicious exercise of their reason.

Which I need not say—by reason of its apparent truth—is the greatest of all God-given faculties. Scarcely a newspaper comes to hand that we do not see in its columns an account of some foolish and wicked quarrel that evidently never would have occurred if the parties to the quarrel had been taught how to reason.

" He who will not reason is a bigot, he who cannot is a fool, and he who dares not is a slave," are words that should be written in gold upon the walls of every school house and prison throughout the length and breadth of the land.

I have been led into this chain of thought, by reading the following pungent and able article by the editor of the *Oakland Times*, which reads as follows: " The handy pistol has got in its work again in the affair of Kennedy-Bohen, at San José. These shootings, as the incidents of personal disputes, are always the result of ignorance and the evidence of barbarism. Men who have never learned how to think, who have no training or logic, who have been guided always by prejudice which never reasons, find themselves in wordy conflict. Neither knows what argument is, so neither is able to intelligently say what he thinks he knows. So, with many words, one man succeeds in saying nothing, and with more words the other says nothing in answering him. Each discovers that he is saying nothing, whereupon he proceeds to rave, curse. swear, and blackguard. The blasphemous challenge is at once accepted by the other, and it is discovered that the two owe their intellectual vacancy and degradation to the habit of substituting denunciation for argument and curses for climaxes. A foolish world laments when they pull their pops and crack away at each other. Rather should the world rejoice that each fool turns fool-killer, for so are decimated the ranks of the flat-heads, whose thinking is done for them by demagogues who make up the substance of the mob, who are the ragged foot soldiers of communism."

Professor J. H. Newman says: "The man who has learned to think, and to reason, and to compare, and to discriminate, and to analyze; who has refined his taste, and formed his judgment, and sharpened his mental vision, will not indeed at once be a lawyer, or a pleader, or an orator, or a statesman, or a physician, or a good landlord, or a man of business, or a soldier, or an engineer, or a chemist, or a geologist, or an antiquarian; but he will be placed in that state of intellect in which he can take up any one of these sciences or callings, or any other for which he has a taste or special talent, with an ease, a grace, a versatility, and a success, to which another is a stranger."

ON DISCRETION.

[ADDISON.]

There are many more shining qualities in the mind of man, but there is none so useful as discretion. It is this, indeed, which gives a value to all the rest: which sets them at work in their proper times and places, and turns them to the advantage of the person who is possessed of them. Without it learning is pedantry and wit impertinence; virtue itself looks like weakness; the best parts only qualify a man to be more sprightly in errors and active to his own prejudices. Discretion does not only make a man the master of his own parts, but of other men's. The discreet man finds out the talents of those he communes with, and knows how to apply them to the proper uses. Accordingly, if we look into particular communities and divisions of men, we may observe that it is the discreet man, not the witty, nor the learned, nor the brave, who guides the conversation and gives measures to society. A man with great talents, but void of discretion, is like Polyphemus in the fable, strong and blind; endued with an irresistible force, which, for want of sight, is of no use to him.

3

Though a man has all other perfections, yet if he wants discretion he will be of no great consequence in the world; on the contrary, if he has this single talent in perfection, and but a common share of others, he may do what he pleases in his particular station in life. At the same time that I think discretion the most useful talent a man can be master of, I look upon *cunning* to be the accomplishment of little, mean, ungenerous minds.

Discretion points out the noblest ends to us, and pursues the most proper and laudable methods of attaining them. Cunning has only private, selfish aims, and sticks at nothing which may make them succeed. Discretion has large and extended views; and like a well formed eye, commands a whole horizon; cunning is a sort of short-sightedness, that discovers the minutest objects which are near at hand, but is not able to discover things at a distance. Discretion, the more it is discovered, gives greater authority to the persons who possess it; cunning, when it is once detected, loses its force, and makes a man incapable of bringing about even those events which he might have done had he passed only for a plain man. Discretion is the perfection of reason, and a guide to us in all the duties of life; cunning is a kind of instinct, that only looks out after our immediate interest and welfare. Discretion is only found in men of strong sense and good understandings; cunning is often to be met with in brutes themselves, and in persons who are but the fewest removes from them. In short, cunning is only the mimic of discretion; and it may pass upon weak men, in the same manner as vivacity is often mistaken for wit, and gravity for wisdom.

SELF-RESPECT.

[SAMUEL SMILES.]

Self-discipline and self-control are the beginning of practical wisdom, and these must have their root in self-respect.

Hope springs from it—hope which is the companion of power and the mother of success; for who hopes strongly has within him the gift of miracles.

The humblest may say: "To respect myself, to develop myself; this is my true duty in life. An integral and responsible part of the great system of society, I owe it to society and to its author not to degrade or destroy either my body, mind, or instincts. On the contrary, I am bound to the best of my power to give to those parts of my constitution the highest degree of perfection possible. "I am not only to suppress the evil but to evoke the good elements in my nature. And as I respect myself so am I equally bound to respect others, as they on their part are bound to respect me."

Hence, mutual respect, justice, and order, of which law becomes the written record and guarantee.

Self-respect is the noblest garment with which a man may clothe himself—the most elevating feeling with which mind can be inspired.

One of Pythagoras' wisest maxims, in his "Golden Verses," is that with which he enjoins the pupil to "reverence himself." Borne up by this high idea, he will not defile his body by sensuality, nor his mind by servile thoughts. This sentiment carried into daily life will be found at the root of all the virtues—cleanliness, sobriety, charity, morality, and religion.

"The pious and just honoring of ourselves," said Milton, "may be thought the radical moisture and fountain-head from whence every laudible and worthy enterprise issues forth."

To think meanly of one's self, is to sink into one's own estimation, as well as in the estimation of others. And as the thoughts are, so will the acts be. Man cannot aspire if he looks down; if he will rise, he must look up. The very humblest may be sustained by the proper indulgence of this feeling.

Poverty itself may be lifted and lighted up by self-respect, and it is truly a noble sight to see a poor man hold himself upright amidst the temptations, and refuse to demean himself by low actions.

THE SCHOOL OF DIFFICULTIES THE BEST INSTRUCTOR.

[SAMUEL SMILES.]

To use the words of Burke, difficulty is a severe instructor, set over us by supreme ordinance of a paternal guardian and instructor, who knows us better than we know ourselves, as he loves us better, too. "He that wrestles with us strengthens our nerves and sharpens our skill; our antagonist is thus our helper."

Without the necessity of encountering difficulty life might be easier, but men would be worthless.

For trials, wisely improved, train the character and teach self-help; thus hardship may often prove the wholesomest discipline for us, though we recognize it not.

When the gallant young Hodson, unjustly removed from his Indian command, felt himself sore pressed down by unmerited calumny and reproach, he yet preserved the courage to say to a friend : "I strive to look the worst boldly in the face, as I would an enemy in the field, and do my appointed work resolutely and to the best of my ability, satisfied that there is reason for all, and that even irksome duties well done bring their own reward, and that if not, still they *are* duties."

The battle of life is, in most cases, fought uphill, and to win it without a struggle were, perhaps, to win it without honor. If there were no difficulties there would be no success; if there were nothing to struggle for there would be nothing to be achieved.

Difficulties may intimidate the weak, but they act only as a wholesome stimulus to men of resolution and valor. All experience of life, indeed, serves to prove that the impediments thrown in the way of human advancement may, for the most part, be overcome by steady, good conduct, honest zeal, activity, perseverance, and, above all, by a determined resolution to surmount difficulties and stand up manfully against misfortune. The school of difficulty is the best school of moral discipline for nations as for individuals. Indeed, the history of all the great and good things that have yet been accomplished by men.

Wherever there is difficulty, the individual man must come out for better, for worse. Encounter with it will train his strength and discipline his skill, heartening him for future effort, as the racer, by being trained to run against the hill, at length courses with facility. The road to success may be steep to climb, and it puts to the proof the energies of him who would reach the summit.

But by experience a man soon learns that obstacles are to be overcome by grappling with them; that the nettle feels as soft as silk when it is boldly grasped; and that the most effective help towards realizing the object proposed is the moral conviction that we can and will accomplish it. Thus difficulties often fall away of themselves before the determination to overcome them. Much will be done if we do but try. Nobody knows what he can do till he has tried; and few try their best till they have been forced to do it. "If I could do such and such a thing," sighs the desponding youth.

But nothing will be done if he only wishes. The desire must ripen into purpose and effort; and one energetic attempt is worth a thousand aspirations. It is these thorny "ifs"—the mutterings of impotence and despair—which so often hedge round the field of possibility, and prevent anything being done or even attempted. A difficulty, said Lord Lyndhurst, is a "thing to be overcome:" grapple with it at once: facility will come with practice, and strength and fortitude with repeated effort.

Thus the mind and character may be trained to an almost perfect discipline, and enabled to act with a grace, spirit, and liberty, almost incomprehensible to those who have not passed through a similar experience. Everything that we learn is the mastery of a difficulty: and the mastery of one helps to the mastery of others.

D'Alembert's advice to the student who complained to him about his want of success in mastering the first elements of mathematics was the right one, "Go on, sir, and faith and strength will come to you."

The danseuse who turns a pirouette, the violinist who plays a sonata, have acquired their dexterity by patient repetition and after many failures.

Carisimi, when praised for the ease and grace of his melodies, exclaimed, "Ah! you little know with what difficulty this ease has been acquired."

Sir Joshua Reynolds, when once asked how long it had taken him to paint a certain picture, replied, "All my life."

Henry Clay, the American orator, when giving advice to young men, thus described to them the secret of his success in the cultivation of his art: "I owe my success in life," said he, "chiefly to one circumstance—that at the age of twenty-seven I commenced, and continued for years, the process of daily reading and speaking upon the contents of some historical or scientific book. These off-hand efforts were made, sometimes in a corn-field, at others in the forest, and not unfrequently in some distant barn, with the horse and the ox for my auditors. It is to this early practice of the art of all arts that I am indebted for the primary and leading impulses that stimulated me onward and have shaped and moulded my whole subsequent destiny."

Curran, the Irish orator, when a youth, had a strong defect in his articulation, and at school he was known as "Stuttering Jack Curran." While he was engaged in the study of the law, and still struggling to overcome his defect, he was stung into eloquence by the sarcasm of a member of a debating club, who characterized him as "Orator Mum," for, like Cowper, when he stood up to speak on a previous occasion, Curran had not been able to utter a word.

The taunt stung him, and he replied in a triumphant speech. This accidental discovery in himself of the gift of eloquence encouraged him to proceed in his studies with renewed energy. He corrected his enunciation by reading aloud, emphatically and distinctly, the best passages in literature for several hours every day, studying his features before a mirror, and adopting a method of gesticulation suited to his rather awkward and ungraceful figure.

He also proposed cases to himself, which he argued with as much care as if he had been addressing a jury. Curran began business with the qualification which Lord Eldon stated to be the first request for distinction, that is, "to be not worth a shilling."

While working his way laboriously at the bar, still oppressed by the diffidence which had overcome him in his debating club, he was on one occasion provoked by the Judge (Robinson) into making a very severe retort. In the case under discussion, Curran observed, that he had never met the law laid down by his lordship in any books in his library. "That may be, sir," said the Judge, in a contemptuous tone, "but I suspect that *your* library is very small." His lordship was notoriously a furious political partisan, the author of several anonymous pamphlets characterized by unusual violence and dogmatism. Curran, aroused by the allusion to his straitened circumstances, replied thus: "It is very true, my lord, that I am poor, and that circumstances have certainly curtailed my library; my books are not numerous, but they are select, and I hope they have been perused with proper disposition. I have prepared myself for this high profession by the study of a few good works rather than by the composition of a great many bad ones. I am not ashamed of my poverty, but I should be ashamed of my wealth could I have stooped to acquire it by servility and corruption. If I rise not to rank I shall at least be honest; and should I ever cease to be so, many an example shows me that an ill-gained elevation, by making me the more conspicuous, would only make me the more universally and the more notoriously contemptible."

William Cobbett's account of how he learned English grammar is full of interest and instruction for all students laboring under difficulties. "I learned grammar," said he, "when I was a private soldier on the pay of sixpence a day. The edge of my berth, or that of my guard-bed, was my seat to study in; my knapsack was my bookcase; a list of books lying on my lap was my writing-table, and the task did not demand anything like a year of my life. I had no money to purchase candle or oil. In winter time it was rarely I could get any evening light but that of the fire, and only my turn even at that. And if I, under such circumstances, and without parent or friend to advise or encourage me, accomplished this undertaking, what excuse can there be for any youth, however poor, however pressed with business, or however circumstanced as to room or other conveniences.

"To buy pen or a sheet of paper I was compelled to forego some portion of food, though in a state of half starvation; I had no moment of time that I could call my own, and I had to read and write amidst the talking, laughing. whistling, brawling of at least half a score of the most thoughtless of men, and that, too, in the hours of their freedom from all control. Think not lightly of the farthing that I had to give now and then for ink. pen, or paper! That farthing was, alas! a great sum to me. I was as tall as I am now; I had great health and great exercise. The whole of the

money not expended for us at market was twopence a week for
each man.

" I remember, and well I may! that on one occasion I, after all
necessary expenses, had, on a Friday, made shift to have a halfpenny in reserve, which I had destined for the purchase of a red
herring in the morning; but when I pulled off my clothes at
night, so hungry then as to be hardly able to endure life, I found
that I had lost my halfpenny! I buried my head under the miserable sheet and rug, and cried like a child. And again I say, if
I, under circumstances like these, could encounter and overcome
this task, is there, can there be, in the whole world, a youth to
find an excuse for the non-performance?"

TEMPER.

[HENRY GILES.]

It is truly astonishing how little our moral reflections dwell
upon our tempers; how seldom the errors of it impress us with any
strong regrets or penitence. We rarely blame ourselves on their
account, and we further presume that others also ought not to
blame us. We value a good reputation beyond riches, and for
fame or fortune we think no exertion too great: but as to the regu-
lation of temper, not to say that we rarely esteem it a duty, we
rarely give it a thought. We do not reflect on the space of existence over which our temper spreads, and which it bathes in light
or sows with thorns. We do not remember how passing cruel we
may be without inflicting wounds of imprisonment, without either
the dagger or the dungeon. We do not think that we are all creatures of sympathy, that we share each other's life, and that we
have a power, all but boundless, to render each other happy or
unhappy. In the strength of our selfishness we too often forget
the harshness of our words, the coldness or bitterness of our looks,
and we care not for the deep and bleeding incisions which they
leave behind them. We do not enough consider how much a
gentle temper may be the evidence of a noble nature; and how
much an ungentle one may be the shadowing forth of a dark and
contracted soul; the moral beauty as well as moral strength that

are implied in sweetness of spirit, and the moral hideousness that makes its dwelling in a bitter heart.

What is the difference in principle between the most cruel tyrant and the truest lover of his kind? It is temper. When your imagination forms to itself the idea of an angel or a fiend, what is still the difference? It is temper. And could you clothe the angel or the fiend in human shape, the most prominent characteristic in each would yet be temper.

As to those also whom we once have known, who casually crossed our path, or walked along with us for years in this, our pilgrimage, does not our involuntary memory turn to their habits of temper?

When their bones are in ashes, when many of their good and bad deeds have gone into forgetfulness, again and again they live to us in the recollection of their tempers; we see again their benign or clouded looks, we hear again their kind or harsh expressions. We can forget an act of malice, however dark, but we cannot forget that which for years has eaten as iron into our souls.

We may be ungrateful for an act of goodness, however generous, but we are unable to dissolve the charm which through many days of peace and charity, spreads its light around us. We consider not how much temper enters into daily life; how it penetrates the whole surface of existence: that it is our daily employments, in our general society, in our homes, around our hearths; that it gives sweetness to the dinner of herbs, or turns luxury to the food of misery.

It would be impossible to enumerate and classify all the failings of temper, for they are as many as there are peculiarities of human character. The general constitution of the mind gives the cast to the temper; and therefore the varieties of temper must be infinite. We shall, however, glance at bad temper in a few of its most evil forms, and we can only do so in some of their broader distinctions. There are the *violent*, strong in coarse and selfish passions, unable to bear any contradiction to a stubborn will, and, as the case may be, they keep in strife a nation or a household. The temper of this species is the prime element in the tyrannic character, whether of greater or smaller dimensions, whether of a family or an empire. Give it a religious direction and it makes the bigot, the fanatic, and the persecutor. Give it power, and it will again open the inquisition, or rekindle the fires of the stake.

In more calm and respectable orders of society, wherever decorum at the least has rule, this disposition can have but rare exhibition; but in other grades of life, in which character has but rude formation and expression, no restraint, it has a ravaging and a fearful existence. It grieves one to the very heart to know that a low, barbarous, and ruffian nature, sulky, obtuse, and unforbearing, can fill to the brim the measure of calamity, that the few he has near him can endure; that the home he calls his castle, he can for others make a dungeon; that the liberty of which he boasts, he can make to them a bondage; that the power which should be their guardianship, he can make their terror; it grieves one, I say, to know that such a savage may exist in a free and Christian country; that he can heap sorrows without number on dependent and defenseless victims; that he can embitter their existence and bruise their hearts; that within his sphere of bounded tyranny, he can be as complete a despot as if he wore the crown of all the Russias—a cruel, fierce, and unmitigated despot.

There are, again, the *morose;* and the temper of this class, as it has various forms, so it has likewise manifold sources. It may be founded in extreme self-consequence, or in extreme self-dissatisfaction, and it may be evidenced in haughty contempt, or in silent and cold indifference. Such a temper constrains the spirit; it leaves the soul few social attractions and few generous desires; it throws gloom where there ought to be light; it withers the smile half formed; it silences the word half spoken; it robs action of loveliness, and takes all grace from speech; it has no soul of frank and generous appreciation; its natural element is to destroy rather than to create: it seems to live only to prove how much a rational creature may mistake the object of his existence, and how much pain one human creature may give to another without reaping any gain or pleasure to himself. The misery that violence inflicts, it inflicts openly—this does it silently; violence often feels its wrong—this never: violence has its moments of deep compunction, and periods of sorrowful and gentle tenderness, that almost atone for many of its worst injuries—but this austere reserve has no visitings of open-heartedness, and no

times of refreshment. I have said that a violent temper makes
the tyrant—this makes the cynic; I have said that a violent
temper makes the fanatic—this makes the ascetic; if both, therefore, be equal in unkindness, the one is at least more coldly intolerable than the other.

Further, there are the *revengeful*. The others I have mentioned
are commonly founded in pride; this more frequently in vanity.
Pride can be magnanimous, can forget, and can forgive; but
wounded vanity remembers an offense forever, and seldom for-
gives it. To beings of this spirit, flattery is the very breath of
their nostrils, the food of their life. Rough or disagreeable truth
is not to be endured; but what, then, must be positive injustice?
Sensitive at all points, such persons are hurt when you do not
know it and could not intend it. Often you give a mortal stab
when you but make a careless movement; they ponder over words
and actions until a mole-hill seems to be a mountain, and they
revolve and revolve the thought so often that an offense becomes
fixed, immovable in their imaginations; they catch the trans-
gressor by the throat and will not let him go until he has paid
the uttermost farthing. In this imperfect world we have many
failings and many provocations, but as we value the least frag-
ment of a benign humanity, let us keep the spirit free from this
most bitter dreg of earthly evils, this last and worst sin of a short-
sighted and corrupt nature. O, let us, as we value our own
heart's best and most godlike peace, as we value every moment
of present tranquillity and of future hope, keep them free from
anti-social and hard and unmerciful dispositions.

There are, moreover, the *discontented*. The temper of these is
that which goes from Dan to Beersheba, and on every step of the
way cries that all is barren. This is the one that sees little in
man or in life with the open heart or clear eye of enjoyment; this
is the one that no society can please, that no character can suit,
that no exertions can earn approval from, that no condition can
satisfy; that is, equally complaining, equally unhappy, equally
dissatisfied, in prosperity or in poverty. For those of such spirit,
earth has no retreat; they can have no shelter and no refuge.
Whither can they flee? The world is full of imperfections, and
so are the men who live in it. If we have only sight for evils,
they are abundant in every place and in all conditions; wherever

we turn, if we will look on aught but these, we must have aching heads and aching souls.

There are persons who seem even to delight in proving that there is in the world more of evil than of good, and more of what is baneful than of what is beautiful. They take joy from prosperity, and they add more than its natural bitterness to poverty; in success they are without gratitude, in failure they are without patience or dignity; to describe them in few words, they are always disappointed. The mountain or the plain, the city or the desert, soft skies or dark ones, are all equal to those who will not see the works of God with a single eye, and will not hear the words of man with an open ear. The glories of nature, or the glories of art, men, books, or business—nothing can take from them the occasion to complain. No gleam from heaven can cheer their hearts, no sounds on earth can charm away their irritation. There is no benison in religion that can give them a contented peace: they wither under a spiritual malady; they are not happy, and, stranger still, they scarcely would be happy. If this be thought an overcolored picture, turn to what we witness daily in life, to what we daily feel in our own minds, the peevish tempers in which we all so constantly indulge, and in which we think it no harm to indulge, the remorseless and ungenerous petulance with which we hurt our fellow creatures, with which we make them suffer for any of our own small vexations or annoyances—vexations or annoyances that we have brought upon ourselves, and which it is more than probable we fully merit. In this most unamiable temper we chill and disgust the best intentioned friends; the movement of kindness is despised: the word of affection dies upon the lips of the utterer; a willingness to think wrong where it is *not*, to *exaggerate* where it is, predominates in such natures; no devotion of attachment, no ardor of generosity, no zeal of love can conquer it. Child or servant lives but in slavery or fear, and often when most deserving receives most rebuke.

Brethren, if our souls are tortured with unknown sorrows, as many of them must be, if we have griefs for which we have no speech, if we have cares with which we cannot trust the stranger, if we have thoughts and woes which we have no heart to tell even to our nearest friends, yet let us not dishonor them, let us not desecrate them by distilling them into the venom of ungenial tempers, let us magnanimously endure them, let us be ourselves the martyrs of our own sufferings; and if we cannot assauge them in our closet by weeping and by prayer, let us not embitter the lot of others by peevishness and by cynicisms. If we cannot be cheerful, let us at least not be unamiable. If we cannot rejoice when others rejoice, let us not throw gall into the cup of pleasure which mortals here are permitted to taste, and which must soon be emptied.

But to observe, as sometimes we all may, the face grow dark, and the tones become harsh, on account of some wretched trifle, some bubble that is to vanish in a moment, we wonder not it should be so, because they are Christians, but because they are rational creatures; we wonder not because they give pain to brethren, but because they ruffle their own peace: and all this for what to either was not worth a moment's trouble or a moment's annoyance.

To close the enumeration we mention the *capricious;* and this is the worst, for it is the most uncertain. You have nothing on which to calculate; you have no means of refuge or of remedy. To the violent and morose, you may oppose patience and thus disarm them; the haughty we may meet with humility, and haply subdue them; the discontented you may learn not to notice; the peevish, if they are worth gaining, or your duty teaches you to make the effort, you may at least gain by proofs of sincerity and tenderness; but of the capricious you have never the slightest security, neither for hatred nor for love. Gentle this hour, they are stern in the next, zealous and indifferent, kindly and severe, indulgent and vindictive, charitable and unmerciful; they run incessantly through all modes of feeling; they exhibit in no long periods of time all possible contrasts of characters; their evil is equally evanescent with their good, but you can never be armed for their evil, and you have no sooner felt their good, than you fear to lose it. At one time they would move heaven and earth to make you happy, and in the turn of a moment they would scarcely move a finger; at one time they would burden you with favors, and at others they heap on you their darkest dislike; to-day they offer you their friendship and to-morrow they withdraw it, and both the offer and the withdrawal are equally without assignable or discoverable reason. Their will is their law, but if there be such a thing, their law is chance. They seem to have no settled rules in either their feelings or their actions, no defined order of character, and, therefore, you have no common principles on which to judge them or by which to hold them. You feel near them, similarly to those who stand around an eastern Sultan's throne—who at one moment bask in the smiles of his favor, but who are in hourly fear he will give the nod which shall unsheath the sword of the executioner.

Those who are in immediate connection with the class that I have described, live in constant and painful alternation, in which there is no ease, or certainly, or comfort; in which life is made such a mortal torture as scarcely to be endured; in which family dependence is a galling yoke, and the bread of toil is eaten in tears of bitterness. Servants in lands of liberty, can retreat, they can choose their masters—but families, what can they do? Remain and suffer; remain, endure, and be hopeless and helpless victims; remain, and for mere existence bear whatever those who rule their existence can heap upon them; remain and have all the pangs of martyrdom and none of its honors. We cannot always choose our lot, nor is it right to quarrel with the lot which is assigned us; but if it were permitted us, there are surely many things which we would prefer to constant irritation and to domestic tyranny. It were better to scoop a cave in an Arabian desert, and, as the old hermits did, diet on herbs and water, than to be under this irritable and cruel caprice, though we should have robes of purple and fare sumptuously every day; it were better to raise a tent in some woods of the far off and untrodden west; it were better to be amidst the wild and pathless prairies, and to take the red man's fate, to have freedom and peace, and communion with God, amidst His most awful solitudes and His grandest works, than to be inmates of a palace in which ill temper were the presiding spirit. Duty might command us to bear, but inclination would never choose it.

I have thus endeavored to point out a few broad generalities. In such a subject, minuteness were impossible. We give no rules for cure, because we conceive all such rules inefficacious. Each one should know his own special temptation, and if he is at all to be corrected, from himself should come the remedy.

It is vain to give rules and maxims; they are of no account,

unless there is an inward feeling of imperfection; unless there is
an earnest, a heartfelt, a conscientious spirit of sincerity; if these
be in the mind, it will truly discover and most earnestly apply the
very best means of moral progression. Still it is right for us to
consider a few of the excuses which are alleged for ill temper.
And when faults of temper are at all admitted, what are the
excuses pleaded? Some plead natural constitution—they are
betrayed, when they design it not, into wrong speaking and into
wrong doing. Some plead bodily illness or the misfortunes of
life; want of health has thrown a cloud upon their spirits, or men
have not dealt well with them, or fortune and the world have been
rough and boisterous on their course; some plead the errors of their
previous training; they were not taught better, and they did not
see better; they were furnished with no right principles, and they
saw all wrong examples. Some plead provocations not to be
resisted, and say that to have been otherwise than they are, were
to have been more than human. Some unwilling to confess any
fault, will maintain that their conduct is that which is just and
necessary. This would, no doubt, be the large class, when they
reason with men; we hope they are not so, when they reason with
their conscience; still, at times, they must remember that although
man sees only the outside appearance, God judges the heart. But
as to these or any other excuses, whilst we should be generous in
admitting them for our brethren, we should be cautious in taking
them to ourselves.

That physical constitution is at the root of many of our faults,
is not to be denied, but neither is it to be denied that it has an
influence on much of our excellence. We know there are those
in earliest youth, whom all of us have had the means of discern-
ing. confiding, faithful, charitable, ready to be pleased, unwilling
to find fault; whilst others have been sharp, harsh, unkind,
watchful, proud, and selfish. And seldom has it been that the
latter nature has been opposed to early promise. That natural
disposition may cause moral derangement should not be denied,
neither should it be excluded from the number of mitigating
circumstances; that illness may depress, and misfortunes vex us,
we are all too well experienced to be severe on those who have
undergone them impatiently; that wrong education may leave
faults which shall endure to the latest hours of life, many of us

have but too much reason to lament, and these faults may be far more sincerely lamented by those who commit them, than by those who condemn them; that great provocation—and much there certainly is in life—demands also charitable allowance, we have no reason and no wish to deny, when it calls forth a strong and indignant burst of passion.

But when we have made all the admission that justice demands and charity can grant, some serious considerations remain, after all, to be pondered. In what way do we use these excuses? How often do we advance them when there is no ground for any of them, when there is no illness, no adversity, no evil example, no evil communication, no resistance; when every word and will is law; when health, and prosperity, and pleasures, and hopes, and friendship, and smiles from heaven and from men, and obsequious attendants are all about us, or awaiting our commands; when the miseries that strike others down have passed over us, and not touched us; when death, the lot of all, as yet has left our dwelling full; when as yet the destroying angel has never waved his sword over us, nor pierced our hearts, nor opened the sluices of our tears; how often then are we in bitter and unhappy moods, when there seems no human reason, but an infatuated perverseness.

And though all these excuses in part were true, how much in our self-love do we over-color them. We are our own advocates, and therefore we are not likely to be just or severe judges. But though they were entirely true, what of that? Is it not demanded of a moral and virtuous man to overcome temptation, to subdue difficulties? Will not the right-minded man, not to say the Christian, struggle against his natural infirmities, nor cease until he has secured a victory? If we were to act on all our merely natural emotions, moral reasoning must be put out of question. Akin to the brutes, we should be driven by the force of impulse, and to this necessity we can neither attach praise nor censure. We call not the gentleness of the lamb *virtue*, nor the fierceness of the tiger *vice*. But man we expect to have a control over his sensations; we expect him to be a moral being, and if he looks to us, not to reckon the wrong he has done, because he has done it in accordance with his sensations; he asks us in point of fact to strip him of his humanity. Similar reasoning applies to the other causes alleged, but not so directly.

We cannot here go into the distinctions; enough is it to say that we have seen them frequently overcome, and what has been done hitherto can be done again. What men *ought* to do they can do, and all excuses to the contrary are but so many equivocations and sophistries for self-will.

It has been the misfortune of many to have received a false training, and to have witnessed unseemly examples, but they have cast off the incubus of their education and been good in spite of their examples. It has been the misfortune of many to lie long and low in sickness, but it has been their glory and their blessing to be meek through all their pains. There have been those who have come to a poor and dependent old age, and yet preserved the affections of their hearts and the light of their spirits; there have been those who have seen their best expectations fail on the point of fulfillment, and their best contrived plans turned into vanity, and their honest exertions defeated, and nothing but losses, struggles, and fears made the daily and nightly companions of their thoughts, who have yet well endured their lot and valiantly fought their fight, who could shake off the dark fiend that haunts the afflicted, who would not hear the voice of the tempter, and cursed neither God nor man. There have been those who, in the teeth of the most violent provocation, thought forbearance more noble than contest; who learned and practiced the magnanimous lesson, "not to return evil for evil," and who preferred rather to endure injury than to inflict it; who would have chosen rather to pray with Christ on his cross than to reign with the wrongdoer on his throne. All these excuses are futile and unsound; we must not deceive ourselves by them. Evil tempers can be corrected, and they ought.

They can be corrected. Who is he that says, he cannot help being angry, or sullen, or peevish? I tell him he deceives himself. We constantly avoid doing so, when our interest or decorum requires it, when we feel near those whom we know are not bound to bear our whims, or who will resent them to our injury; but what strangers will not endure we cast upon our friends. That temper can be corrected, the world proves by thousands of instances. There have been those who set out in life with being

4

violent. peevish, discontented, irritable, and capricious, whom thought, reflection, effort, not to speak of piety, have rendered, as they became mature, meek, peaceful, loving, generous, forbearing, tranquil, and consistent. It is a glorious achievement, and blessed is he who attains it.

But taking the argument to lower ground, which I do unwillingly, you continually see men controlling their emotions, when their interest commands it. Observe the man who wants assistance, who looks for patronage, how well, as he perceives coldness, does he crush the vexation that rises in his throat, and stifle the indignation that burns for expression. How will the most proud and lofty descend from their high position, and lay aside their ordinary bearing, to earn a suffrage from the meanest kind. And surely those who hang around us in life, those who lean on us, or on whom we lean through our pilgrimage, to whom our accents and our deeds are worlds, to whom a word may shoot a pang worse than the stroke of death, surely I say, if we can do so much for interest, we can do something for goodness and for gratitude. And in all civilized intercourse, how perfectly do we see it ourselves to be the recognized law of decorum, and if we have not universally good feelings, we have generally, at least, good manners. This may be hypocrisy, but it ought to be sincerity, and we trust it is.

If, then, we can make our faces to shine on strangers, why darken them on those who should be dear to us? Is it that we have so squandered our smiles abroad, that we have only frowns to carry home? Is it that while out in the world, we have been so prodigal of good temper, that we have but our ill humors with which to cloud our firesides? Is it, that it requires often but a mere passing guest to enter, while we are speaking daggers to beings who are nearest to us in life, to change our tone, to give us perfect self-command, that we cannot do for love, what we do for appearance? Brethren, we can rule our tempers, and we ought.

THE EVILS WHICH FLOW FROM UNRESTRAINED PASSIONS.

[BLAIR.]

When man revolted from his Maker, his passions rebelled against himself, and from being originally the ministers of reason, have become the tyrants of the soul. Hence, in treating of this subject, two things may be assumed as principles: first, that, through the present weakness of the understanding, our passions are often directed towards improper objects; and next, that even when their direction is just, and their objects are innocent, they perpetually tend to run into excess; they always hurry us towards their gratification, with a blind and dangerous impetuosity. On these two points, then, turns the whole government of our passions: first, to ascertain the proper object of their pursuit; and next, to restrain them in that pursuit, when they would carry us beyond the bounds of reason. If there is any passion which intrudes itself unseasonably into our mind, which darkens and troubles our judgment, or habitually discomposes our temper, which unfits us for properly discharging the duties, or disqualifies us for cheerfully enjoying the comforts of life, we may certainly conclude it to have gained a dangerous ascendant. The great object which we ought to propose to ourselves is, to acquire a firm and steadfast mind, which the infatuation of passions shall not seduce nor its violence shake; which, resting on fixed principles, shall, in the midst of contending emotions, remain free, and master of itself; able to listen calmly to the voice of conscience, and prepared to obey its dictates without hesitation.

To obtain, if possible, such command of passion is one of the highest attainments of the rational nature. Arguments to show its importance crowd upon us from every quarter. If there be any fertile source of mischief to human life, it is, beyond doubt, the misrule of passion. It is this which poisons the enjoyment of individuals, overturns the order of society, and strews the path of life with so many miseries, as to render it, indeed, the vale of tears. All those great scenes of public calamity, which we behold with astonishment and horror, have originated from the source of violent passions. These have overspread the earth with bloodshed. These have pointed the assassin's dagger and filled the poisoned bowls. These, in every age, have furnished too copious materials for the orator's pathetic declamations, and for the poet's tragical song.

When from public life we descend to private conduct, though passion operates not there in so wide and destructive a sphere, we shall find its influence to be no less baneful. I need not mention the black and fierce passions, such as envy, jealousy, and revenge, whose effects are obviously noxious, and whose agitations are immediate misery. But take any of the licentious kind. Suppose it to have unlimited scope; trace it through its course; and we shall find that gradually, as it rises, it taints the soundness and troubles the peace of his mind over whom it reigns; that, in its progress, it engages him in pursuits which are marked either with danger or with shame; that, in the end, it wastes his fortune, destroys his health, or debases his character; and aggravates all the miseries in which it has involved him, with the concluding pangs of bitter remorse. Through all the stages of this fatal course, how many have heretofore run? What multitudes do we daily behold pursuing it, with blind and headlong steps.

TOLERANCE.

[CHESTERFIELD.]

Remember that errors and mistakes, however gross in matters of opinion, if they are sincere, are to be pitied, but not punished nor laughed at. The blindness of the understanding is as much to be pitied as the blindness of the eyes; and there is neither jest nor guilt in a man losing his way in either case. Charity bids us set him right if we can by arguments and persuasions; but charity, at the same time, forbids either to punish or ridicule his misfortunes. Every man's reason is and must be his guide; and I may as well expect that every man should be of my size and complexion as that he should reason just as I do.

Every man seeks for truth, but God only knows who has found it. It is, therefore, as unjust to persecute as it is absurd to ridicule people for their several opinions, which they cannot help entertaining upon the conviction of their reason. It is the man who tells, or who acts a lie, that is guilty, and not he who honestly and sincerely believes the lie.

GOOD-BREEDING.

[CHESTERFIELD.]

Civility and good-breeding are generally thought, and often used, as synonymous terms, but are by no means so.

Good-breeding necessarily implies civility, but civility does not reciprocally imply good-breeding. The former has its intrinsic weight and value, which the latter always adorns, and often doubles, by its workmanship. To sacrifice one's own self-love to other people's is a short, but I believe, a true definition of civility; to do it with ease, propriety, and grace, is good-breeding. The one is the result of good nature; the other of good sense, joined to experience, observation, and attention.

A plowman will be civil, if he is good natured, but cannot be well-bred. A courtier will be well-bred, though perhaps without good nature, if he has but good sense. Flattery is the disgrace of good-breeding, as brutality often is of truth and sincerity. Good-breeding is the middle point between these two odious extremes. Ceremony is the superstition of good-breeding, as well as of religion; but yet, being an outwork to both, should not be absolutely demolished. It is always to a certain degree to be complied with, though despised, by those who think, because admired and respected by those who do not.

Good-breeding, like charity, not only covers a multitude of faults, but, to a certain degree, supplies the want of some virtue. In the common intercourse of life, it acts good nature, and often does what good nature will not always do; it keeps both wits and fools within the bounds of decency, which the former are too apt to transgress, and which the latter never know.

I would not be misapprehended and supposed to recommend good-breeding, thus profaned and prostituted to the purposes of guilt and perfidy; but I think I may justly infer from it, to what a degree the accomplishment of good-breeding must adorn and enforce virtue and truth, when it can thus soften the outrages and deformity of vice and falsehood.

I observe with concern, that it is the fashion for our youth of both sexes to brand good-breeding with the name of ceremony and formality. As such, they ridicule and explode it, and adopt in its stead an offensive carelessness and inattention, to the diminution, I will venture to say, even of their own pleasures, if they know what true pleasures are.

Love and friendship necessarily produces, and justly authorize familiarity; but then good-breeding must mark out its bounds, and thus far shalt thou go, and no further; for I have known many a passion and many a friendship degraded, weakened, and at last, if I may use the expression, wholly slatterned away, by an unguarded and illiberal familiarity. Nor is good-breeding less the ornament and cement of common social life; it connects, it endears, and at the same time that it indulges the just liberty, restrains that indecent licentiousness of conversation, which alienates and provokes. Great talents make a man famous, great merit makes him respected, and great learning makes him esteemed; but good-breeding alone can make him loved. Upon the whole, though good-breeding cannot, strictly speaking, be called a virtue, yet it is productive of so many good effects, that in my opinion, it may justly be reckoned more than a mere accomplishment.

MANNERS AND MORALS.

[SAMUEL SMILES.]

Dr. Johnson has said that the habit of looking at the best side of a thing is worth more to a man than a thousand pounds a year. And we possess the power, to a great extent, of so exercising the will as to direct the thought upon objects calculated to yield happiness and improvement rather than their opposites.

In this way the habit of happy thought may be made to spring up like any other habit.

And to bring up men or women with a genial nature of this sort, a good temper, and a happy frame of mind, is, perhaps, of even more importance in many cases than to perfect them in much knowledge and many accomplishments.

As daylight can be seen through very small holes, so little things illustrate a person's character. Indeed, character consists in little acts, well and honorably performed; daily life being the quarry from which we build up and rough-hew the habits which form it.

One of the most marked tests of character is the manner in which we conduct ourselves towards others. A graceful behavior towards superiors, inferiors, and equals is a constant source of pleasure. It pleases others because it indicates respect for their personalities, but it gives tenfold more pleasure to ourselves. Every man may, to a large extent, be a self-educator in good behavior, as in everything else; he can be civil and kind, if he will, though he have not a penny in his purse.

Gentleness in society is like the silent influence of light, which gives color to all nature; it is far more powerful than loudness or force and far more fruitful. It pushes its way quietly and persistently, like the tiniest daffodil in spring, which raises the clod and thrusts it aside by the simple persistency of growing. Even a kind look will give pleasure and confer happiness. In one of Robertson Brighton's letters he tells of a lady who related to him the delight, the tears of gratitude, which she had witnessed in a poor girl to whom, in passing, "I gave a kind look on going out of church on Sunday." What a lesson! How cheaply happiness can be given! What opportunities we miss of doing an angel's work! I remember doing it, full of sad feelings, passing on, and thinking no more about it, and it gave an hour's sunshine to a human life and lightened the load of life to a human heart for a time.

Morals and manners, which give color to life, are of much greater importance than laws, which are but their manifestations. The law touches us here and there, but manners are about us everywhere, pervading society like the air we breathe. Good manners, as we call them, are neither more nor less than good behavior; consisting of courtesy and kindness; benevolence being the preponderating element in all kinds of mutually beneficial and pleasant intercourse amongst human beings.

"Civility," said Lady Montague, "costs nothing and buys every-thing."

The cheapest of all things is kindness, its exercise requiring the least possible trouble and self-sacrifice.

"Win hearts," said Burleigh to Queen Elizabeth, "and you have all men's hearts and purses."

If we would only let nature act kindly, free from affectation and artifice, the results on social good humor and happiness would be incalculable.

The little courtesies which form the small change of life, may separately appear of little intrinsic value, but they acquire their importance from repetition and accumulation. They are like the spare minutes, or the groat a day, which proverbially produce such momentous results in the course of a twelvemonth, or in a life time.

Manners are the ornament of action, and there is a way of speaking a kind word, or of doing a kind thing, which greatly enhances its value.

What seems to be done with a grudge, or as an act of condescension, is scarcely accepted as a favor. Yet there are men who pride themselves upon their gruffness, and though they may possess virtue and capacity, their manner is often such as to render them almost insupportable.

It is difficult to like a man who, though he may not pull your nose habitually, wounds your self-respect, and takes a pride in saying disagreeable things to you. There are others who are dreadfully condescending, and cannot avoid seizing upon every small opportunity of making their greatness felt.

When Abernethy was canvassing for the office of Surgeon to St. Bartholomew's Hospital, he called upon such a person—a rich grocer, one of the Governors. The great man behind the counter, seeing the great surgeon enter, immediately assumed the grand air towards the supposed suppliant for his vote. "I presume, sir, you want my vote and interest at this momentous epoch of your life."

Abernethy, who hated humbugs, and felt nettled at the tone, replied: "No, I don't; I want a pennyworth of figs; come, look sharp, and wrap them up; I want to be off."

The cultivation of manners—though in excess it is foppish and foolish—is highly necessary in a person who has occasion to negotiate with others in matters of business. Affability and good breeding may even be regarded as essential to the success of a man in any eminent station and enlarged sphere of life; for the want of it has not unfrequently been found in a great measure to neutralize the result of much industry, integrity, and honesty of character. There are, no doubt, a few strong tolerant minds which can bear with defects and angularities of manners, and look only to the more genuine qualities; but the world at large is not so forbearant, and cannot help forming its judgments and likings mainly according to outward conduct.

Another mode of displaying true politeness is consideration for the opinions of others. It has been said of dogmatism, that it is only puppyism come to its full growth; and certainly the worst form this quality can assume is that of opinionativeness and arrogance.

Let men agree to differ, and when they do differ, bear and forbear. Principles and opinions may be maintained with perfect suavity, without coming to blows or uttering hard words; and there are circumstances in which words are blows, and inflict wounds far less easy to heal. As bearing upon this point, we quote an instructive little parable spoken some time since by an itinerant preacher of the Evangelical Alliance on the borders of Wales. "As I was going to the hills," said he, "early one misty morning, I saw something moving on a mountain side so strange looking that I took it for a monster. When I came nearer to it I found it was a man. When I came up to him I found he was my brother."

The inbred politeness which springs from right-heartedness and kindly feelings is of no exclusive rank or station. The mechanic who works at the bench may possess it, as well as the clergyman or the peer. It is by no means a necessary condition of labor that it should, in any respect, be either rough or coarse. The politeness and refinement which distinguish all classes of the people in many continental countries show that those qualities might become ours, too—as doubtless they will become with increased culture and more general social intercourse—without sacrificing any of our more genuine qualities as men. From the highest to the lowest, the richest to the poorest, to no rank or condition in life has nature denied her highest boon—the great heart. There never yet existed a gentleman but was lord of a great heart; and this may exhibit itself under the hodden gray of the peasant as well as under the laced coat of the noble. Robert Burns was once taken to task by a young Edinburgh blood, with whom he was walking, for recognizing an honest farmer in the open street. "Why, you fantastic gomeral," exclaimed Burns, "it was not the great coat, the scone bonnet, and the saundersboot hose that I spoke to, but *the man* that was in them; and the man, sir, for true worth, would weigh down you and me, and ten more such, any day." There may be a homeliness in externals which may seem vulgar to those who cannot discern the heart beneath, but, to the right-minded, character will always have its clear insignia.

LYING.

[CHESTERFIELD.]

There is one vice into which people of good education, and, in the main of good principles, sometimes fall, from mistaken notions of skill, dexterity, and self-defense: I mean lying; though it is inseparably attended with more infamy and loss than any other. The prudence and necessity of concealing the truth, insensibly seduces people to violate it. It is the only art of mean capacities, and the only refuge of mean spirits. Whereas concealing the truth, upon proper occasions, is as prudent and as innocent, as telling a lie, upon any occasion, is infamous and foolish. I will state you a case in your own department:

Suppose you are employed at a foreign court, and that the Minister of that court is absurd or impertinent enough to ask you what your instructions are; will you tell him a lie, which, as soon as found out (and found out it certainly will be) must destroy your credit, blast your character, and render you useless there? No. Will you tell him the truth then, and betray your trust? As certainly no. But you will answer with firmness, that you are surprised at such a question; that you are persuaded he does not expect an answer to it; but that at all events, he certainly will not have one. Such an answer will give him confidence in you; he will conceive an opinion of your veracity, of which opinion you may afterwards make very honest and fair advantages. But if, in negotiations, you are looked upon as a liar and a trickster, no confidence will be placed in you, nothing will be communicated to you, you will be in the situation of a man who has been burnt in the cheek, and who, from that mark, cannot afterwards get an honest livelihood if he would, but must continue a thief.

Lord Bacon, very justly, makes a distinction between simulation and dissimulation; and allows the latter rather than the former, but still observes that they are the weaker sort of politicians who have recourse to either.

A man who has strength of mind, and strength of parts, wants neither of them. "Certainly," says he, "the ablest men that ever were have all had an openness and frankness of dealing, and a name of certainty and veracity; but, then, they were like horses well managed, for they could tell, passing well, when to stop, or turn; and at such times as they thought the case, indeed, required some dissimulation, if then they used it, it came to pass, that the former opinion spread abroad of their good faith and clearness of dealing made them almost invisible."

There are people who indulge themselves in a sort of lying, which they reckon innocent, and which in one sense is so; for it hurts nobody but themselves.

This sort of lying is the spurious offspring of vanity, begotten upon folly; these people deal in the marvelous; they have seen other things which they really never saw, though they did exist, only because they were thought worth seeing. Has anything remarkable been said or done in any place, or in any company, they immediately present and declare themselves eye or ear-witness of it. They have done feats themselves, unattempted, or at least unperformed, by others. They are always the heroes of their own fables, and think that they gain consideration, at least attract attention, by it. Whereas, in truth, all they get is ridicule and contempt, not without a good degree of distrust; for one must naturally conclude, that he who will tell any lie from idle vanity will not scruple telling a greater for interest.

Had I really seen anything so very extraordinary as to be almost incredible, I would keep it to myself, rather than, by telling it, give any one body room to doubt for one minute of my veracity.

It is most certain, that the reputation of chastity is not so necessary for a woman, as that of veracity is for a man, and with reason; for it is possible for a woman to be virtuous, though not strictly chaste, but it is not possible for a man to be virtuous without strict veracity. The slips of the poor women are sometimes mere bodily frailties; but a lie in a man is a vice of the mind and of the heart. For God's sake, be scrupulously jealous of the purity of your moral character! Keep it immaculate, unblemished, unsullied; and it will be unsuspected.

Defamation and calumny never attack, where there is no weak place; they magnify, but they do not create. * * * I really know nothing more criminal, more mean, and more ridiculous, than lying. It is the production either of malice, or cowardice, or vanity; and generally misses of its aim in every one of these views; for lies are always detected sooner or later. If I tell a malicious lie, in order to affect any man's fortune or character, I may indeed injure him for some time; but I shall be sure to be the greatest sufferer myself at last; for as soon as ever I am detected (and detected I most certainly shall be), I am blasted for the infamous attempt; and whatever is said afterwards to the disadvantage of that person, however true, passes for calumny. If I lie or equivocate (for it is the same thing), in order to excuse myself for something I have said or done, and to avoid the danger or shame that I apprehend from it, I discover at once my fear, as well as my falsehood; and only increase instead of avoiding the danger and the shame; I show myself to be the lowest and the meanest of mankind, and am sure to be always treated as such.

Fear, instead of avoiding invites danger; for concealed cowards will insult known ones.

If one has had the misfortune to be in the wrong, there is something noble in frankly owning it. It is the only way of atoning for it, and the only way of being forgiven.

Equivocating, evading, or shuffling, in order to remove a present danger or inconvenience, is something so mean, and betrays so much fear, that whoever practices them always deserves to be and often will be kicked. There is another sort of lies, inoffensive enough in themselves but wonderfully ridiculous; I mean those lies which a mistaken vanity suggests, that defeat the very end for which they are calculated, and terminate in the humiliation and confusion of their author, who is sure to be detected. These are chiefly narrative and historical lies, all intended to do infinite honor to their author.

He is always the hero of his own romances; he has been in dangers from which nobody but himself ever escapes; he has seen with his own eyes, whatever other people have heard or read of; he has had more *bonnes fortunes* than any one else, and has ridden by more mile-posts in one day than ever courier went in two.

He is soon discovered, and as soon becomes the object of universal contempt and ridicule.

Remember, then, as long as you live, that nothing but strict truth can carry you through the world, with either your confidence or your honor unwounded.

It is not only your duty, but your interest; as a proof of which you may always observe, that the greatest fools are the greatest liars.

For my own part, I judge of every man's truth by his degree of understanding.

FRIENDSHIP.

[CHESTERFIELD.]

People of your age have, commonly, an unguarded frankness about them, which makes them the easy prey and bubbles of the artful and the experienced: they look upon every knave or fool who tells them that he is their friend, to be really so; and pay that profession of simulated friendship, with an indiscreet and unbounded confidence, always to their loss, often to their ruin. Beware, therefore, now that you are coming into the world, of these proffered friendships. Receive them with great civility, but with great incredulity too, and pay them with compliments but not with confidence.

Do not let your vanity and self-love make you suppose that people become your friends at first sight, or even upon a short acquaintance. Real friendship is a slow grower, and never thrives, unless ingrafted upon a stock of known and reciprocal merit.

There is another kind of nominal friendship among young people, which is warm for the time, but, by good luck, of short duration.

This friendship is hastily produced, by their being accidentally thrown together, and pursuing the same course of riot and debauchery. A fine friendship, truly! and well cemented by drunkenness and lewdness. It should rather be called a conspiracy against morals and good manners, and be punished as such by the civil magistrate.

However, they have the impudence and the folly to call this confederacy a friendship.

Remember to make a great difference between companions and friends; for a very complaisant and agreeable companion may, and often does, prove a very improper and a very dangerous friend. People will in a great degree, and not without reason, form their opinion of you upon that which they have of your friends; and there is a Spanish proverb, which says very justly, "Tell me whom you live with, and I will tell you who you are."

One may fairly suppose that a man who makes a knave or a fool his friend has something very bad to do or conceal. But at the same time that you carefully decline the friendship of knaves and fools, if it can be called friendship, there is no occasion to make either of them your enemies, wantonly and unprovoked, for they are numerous bodies, and I would rather choose a secure neutrality than alliance or war with either of them. You may be a declared enemy to their views and follies without being marked out by them as a personal one. Their enmity is the next dangerous thing to their friendship.

Have a real reserve with almost everybody, and have a seeming reserve with almost nobody; for it is very disagreeable to seem reserved, and very dangerous not to be so. Few people find the medium; many are ridiculously mysterious and reserved upon trifles, and many imprudently communicative of all they know. * * * I must be first well acquainted with my folks; I will have no friend who is void of sentiment merely because he has wit, nor will I have a sentimental friend who wants common sense. There must be sentiment on both sides to form a friendship, but there must be sense on both sides to carry it on.

RESISTANCE TO TEMPTATION.

[SAMUEL SMILES.]

The young man, as he passes through life, advances through a long line of tempters ranged on either side of him; and the inevitable effect of yielding is degradation in a greater or less degree. Contact with them tends insensibly to draw away from him some portion of the divine electric element with which his nature is charged; and his only mode of resisting them is to utter and to act out his "No," manfully and resolutely. He must decide at once, not waiting to deliberate and balance reasons; for the youth, like "the woman who deliberates is lost." Many deliberate without deciding, but "not to resolve *is* to resolve." A perfect knowledge of man is in the prayer "Lead us not into temptation." But temptation will come to try the young man's strength; and once yielded to, the power to resist grows weaker and weaker. Yield once, and a portion of virtue has gone. Resist manfully, and the first decision will give strength for life; repeated, it will become a habit. It is in the outworks of the habits formed in early life that the real strength of the defense must lie; for it has been wisely ordained that the machinery of moral existence should be carried on principally through the medium of the habits, so as to save the wear and tear of the great principles within. It is good habits, which insinuate themselves into the thousand inconsiderable acts of life, that really constitute by far the part of man's moral conduct.

Hugh Miller has told how by an act of youthful decision he saved himself from one of the strong temptations so peculiar to a life of toil.

When employed as a mason, it was usual for his fellow workmen to have an occasional treat of drink, and one day two glasses of whisky fell to his share, which he swallowed.

When he reached home he found, on opening his favorite book—"Bacon's Essays"—that the letters danced before his eyes, and that he could no longer master the sense. "The condition," he says, "into which I had brought myself was, I felt, one of degradation. I had sunk, by my own act, to a lower level of intelligence than that on which it was my privilege to be placed; and though the state could have been no very favorable one for forming a very favorable resolution, I in that hour determined that I should never sacrifice my capacity of intellectual enjoyment to a drinking usage; and, with God's help, I was enabled to hold by the determination."

It is such decisions as this that often form the turning points in a man's life, and furnish the foundation of his future character.

And this rock, on which Hugh Miller might have been wrecked, if he had not at the right moment put forth his moral strength to strike away from it, is one that youth and manhood alike need to be constantly on their guard against. It is about one of the worst and most deadly as well as extravagant temptations which lie in the way of youth.

Sir Walter Scott used to say that, "Of all vices, drinking is the most incompatible with greatness." Not only so, but it is incompatible with economy, decency, health, and honest living. When a youth cannot restrain, he must abstain.

Dr. Johnson's case is the case of many. He said, referring to his own habits: "Sir, I can abstain; but I can't be moderate." Permit me to add, in connection with the above, that all our danger lies in the *first* drink. And for the reason that, just in proportion to our indulgence, just in proportion will our appetites for strong liquor increase, and *our power of resistance weaken.*

MISCELLANEOUS.

"Put not your faith in Princes," or in the man who "stoops to conquer;" or in the man who says *yes* merely to accommodate you, or in the man who "has a hand for everybody, and a heart for nobody."

Watch the man who treats you well, and see in what manner he treats others; as it is possible he may have a selfish motive in treating you kindly. But when you see that he is as true to others as he is to yourself, then give him your entire confidence, and be as true to him as the "needle is to the pole."—*Ed.*

Be careful what you read, and how you read. A New York journalist says: "I am paid $10,000 a year for keeping the truth out of the journal upon which I am employed." And Professor Mathews says, " Mr. Froude confesses that in historical inquiries the most instructed thinkers have but a limited advantage over the most illiterate."

Those who know the most, whose investigations are the profoundest, approach least to agreement.

" It is probable," says an able Scottish writer, " that *not one fact* in the whole range of history original and derived is truly stated."

Read not to contradict and confute, nor to believe and take for granted, nor to find talk and discourse, but to weigh and consider.
This is the great secret both of reading to profit and of making the best choice of what we read.
If books were more commonly judged by their real weight, how many popular works would sink into insignificance! It is melancholy to think of the millions of immortal minds, that accustom themselves to reading, which when weighed in the balance is found to contain little less than the lightness of vanity. How many that might have attained the stature of full grown man, have thus become enervated, dwarfish, deformed, or crippled. With desires formed for the highest enjoyments and understandings, capable of the noblest improvement, the reading of trifling and pernicious books, the habit of mental association with low, mean, and unworthy thoughts, has prostrated the energies of thousands, and debased them below themselves.—*Lord Bacon.*

Those who have read everything are thought to understand everything too; but it is not always so.
Reading furnishes the mind with only materials of knowledge; it is thinking that makes what we read ours.
We are of the ruminating kind, and it is not enough to cram ourselves with a great load of collections; unless we chew them over again, they will not give us strength and nourishment.— *John Locke.*

The Indian " sees God in clouds and hears Him in the wind," and civilized man, when in a demoralized condition, oftentimes is struck with the divine attributes of his Maker, by looking upon a simple flower. And I was forcibly reminded of the fact a few

5

days since, by hearing one of your fellow-prisoners exclaim, upon seeing a bouquet of flowers upon the desk in the Prison Library, "If there is one thing more than another which brings me near to God, it is flowers."—*Ed.*

Dick Fellows, one of your fellow-prisoners, says, "The Devil oftentimes appears to us in the most attractive form; he appeared to our Saviour on the Mount, in the form of a beautiful woman; and he appeared to me in the form of Wells and Fargo's treasure box."—*Ed.*

"In seasons of distress or difficulty, to abandon ourselves to dejection, carries no mark of a great or a worthy mind. Instead of sinking under trouble, and declaring, 'that his soul is weary of life,' it becomes a wise and a good man, in the evil day, with firmness to maintain his post; to bear up against the storm; to have recourse to those advantages which in the worst of times are always left to integrity and virtue; and never to give up the hope that better days may yet arrive."

Henry Giles, in his essay on "The Weariness of Life," says: "Much of dissatisfaction with life arises from a doubly false estimate of life. We underrate our own position in it; we overrate the position of others. Out of this doubly false estimate spring correspondent false contrasts and desires.

"The man of bodily labor, longs for mental labor; and contrasted with his own condition, he thinks it one of perfect ease.

"And yet with this wish much is often connected that is strange and inconsistent.

"You will sometimes hear a man whose toil is physical, expatiate, with emphasis, upon the comparative idleness which the man enjoys whose avocation is intellectual. Yet the man who thus expatiates on the scholar's indolence, finds it a painful task to write a simple letter on the plainest incidents of domestic history; not because he wants ability or intelligence, but because the use of his mind in this way is unfamiliar to him.

"The fact is, the scholar would have as much reason to dwell on the case of the farmer, as the farmer on the case of the scholar; and so he constantly does, and with just as much of falsehood.

"The scholar contrasts his position falsely with the farmer's by looking from his own confinement to the farmer's exercise.

"The farmer contrasts his position falsely with that of the scholar, by looking from his own muscular exertion to the scholar's muscular repose. But he heeds not the paleness of the student's cheek, or the glisten of his eye, which shows that his retreat has been no fair elysian bower.

"He heeds not the anxieties, the fears, the leaden hours of prolonged exertion which the library door shuts in.

"The man of private life desires the distinctions of public office: but he thinks of its power separate from its toil; of its splendor, separate from its danger; of the glory of success, separate from the shame of defeat; and of the brilliancy of its outward show, separate from the gnawings of its concealed vexations.

"He sees not these agitated hours that are hidden from the world; and he feels not these troubles that, though never uttered, cause the sick heart to heave with uneasy palpitations.

"He does not consider that to widen a man's relations is frequently to multiply his enemies; that to place him in a state which many desire to obtain, is to place him in a position which many will endeavor to embarrass, which many will endeavor to render miserable; that is to place him in a position exposed to envy, jealousy, misrepresentation, and strife; and that all the torments will haunt it which it is in the power of ambitious rivalry or disappointed competition to invoke.

"These things, I am aware, have been said thousands of times before; they will be said thousands of times again; for though life changes in many things as man grows older in history, yet, n many things, life is but the repetition of itself.

"These things, it may be said, are truisms, an old story: and so they are; but life also is a truism, an old story.

"The statement of these mistakes is old, but they are in individuals the occasion of a practical life that is ever varied and is ever new. By underrating, for instance, our own position, we want that spring of hope which is the inspiration of success, and we work in it with feeble and despondent souls.

"We never come to understand the resources it contained, and therefore we never draw out from them the riches which they might have yielded.

" By overrating the position that is *not* ours, our thoughts are divided and our efforts are unsteady. We do not labor with all our heart and strength in our assigned vocation, and frequently we are induced to leave it, to lose all the power which we expended in it, to begin awkwardly in a new direction, to compete with rivalry in ways for which we are not trained; and thus, doubly wasted, doubly impoverished, we fail of all, and in the end grumble with our lot and quarrel with our life."

Putting on Good Manners with Sunday Clothes.

Whilst it is the duty of every man in civilized society to pay a proper regard to his personal appearance, it is the height of folly for one to think that gentility can be put on or off with our Sunday clothes. As well might the ape attempt to assume the dignified appearance of the philosopher, or the San Francisco hoodlum to put on good clothes with the view of the clothes covering from sight his uncouth and disgusting manners, as for us to suppose for a moment that we can play the part of blackguard six days in the week and appear like a gentleman on the seventh.—*Ed.*

HE'S LOST HIS GRIP.

The following sketch, from the pen of Prentice Mulford, will be read with deep interest by those who have given up all hope of being able to improve their condition:

"It used to be said of a man in the mines, when he became discouraged, downcast, and disinclined to labor, plan, or project, and very much inclined to get drunk whenever he had a chance, 'he lost his grip.'

"There seems a great deal of hidden meaning and force in many of these phases which are evolved, not of dictionaries or the closets of pedants, but from the situations, necessities, emergencies, and results of every-day life.

"Because a hopeful or energetic man or woman, full of enterprise and plan, takes a firmer hold or grip on life. You may see it in their resolute walk and carriage, by the manner in which each footstep is planted, and when they shake hands with you they take your hand as if they meant something by it.

" It seems to me that getting this 'grip' on life is yet an untaught science; that there is a quality of the mind born of resolution and decision, whereby this grip is maintained; that it is of vast importance it should be better understood and comprehended; that disease and weakness, first mental, next physical, comes of losing this grip, and that is a matter to be considered, both with reference to the 'here' and the hereafter.

" I think a good 'grip' on life will help to cure almost any failing and any disease. Doctors will tell you, and many of us know of people, who ought to have died, according to all the rules of medical science, long ago, but who wouldn't die because they said they wouldn't, and they didn't. They never let go their 'grip' on life.

" It is wonderful what a strengthening effect a word may have on a person's mind as regards holding his 'grip.' You say to yourself in times of difficulty, doubt, and discouragement, ' I will,' ' I will,' ' I will ' do thus and so, and keep on from time to time repeating these words, and you seem to call into yourself at last a power—a power of which helps remove the trouble. You laugh, of course, at this, and say, ' that's all imagination.' Of course. Laugh away. It will do you good. But try the recipe the next time you want to climb out of the dumps. Say, ' I will climb out of this mire.' Keep on saying it. See if it does not help you to climb.

" You need so to climb, perhaps, for your heart is heavy, your body weak, your will ditto, your appetite gone, the world a vale of tears, and life a burden. A 'heavy heart' means literally and physically, a heavy and cast-down heart, for if you could examine that useful organ at such times, you might find it below its proper place; that it was not pumping blood with its accustomed energy, and that the blood about it was more or less congested and of sluggish motion, all of which causes give that peculiar pain and heaviness, known as a 'headache.' Of course, if the heart does not work properly neither will the stomach, and if the stomach does not work, what will work inside of us? Our organs are much like a row of bricks—upset one and the rest follow suit.

" It is very important that things do work properly inside of us, in order that we may properly work things outside.

" What is grip? Call it will. What is will? I do not know. It is a quality of which each person has more or less. It is a very desirable quality. A person having it in plenty and knowing it, and knowing the necessity for its use, can do a great deal in the world. The will is put in as a power, and there is good reason to believe that it may be increased by cultivation, or by willing to have more will. There is reason to believe that its capacity for increase is illimitable. Whether it so grows inside of us, or whether it is an element we draw to us from the outside, I cannot say and never found anybody who could. But if it can be cultivated and increased by so easy and simple a process as wishing for more of it, asking for it, praying for it, demanding it and saying ' I will,' it is a very important thing for people to know.

" Please do not be too ready to ' despise the day of small things.' We know really very little of these thinking mysteries we call our minds. If you declared to another your belief that a thought was a thing—an invisible thing, to be sure, but none the less a thing— an element or combination of elements coming out of your brain maybe, you would be met with a howl of derision. The idea that thoughts are things—are anything! Thought, the mind, pictures, plans, opinions, wishes, lies, half-lies, and all the product of our minds are only myths—nothings—of course. We can't see them; hence, they are nothings or next to it. So we reason in this matter.

" Yet it's the thought that does it all. You plan—you think out your undertaking, first, and then put it in practice afterwards. You plan, first, every physical act, even to each step made in walking. When you say, ' I will,' or ' I won't,' and put your mental foot down with energy and decision on this ' say so' you do create something about you which seems to make more energy, decision, and resolution—more power to perform the ' I will,' or ' I won't.'

" Why, the lack of ' grip' will write itself all over people's forms and faces. You know the man who has ' lost his grip' by the pursed lips, the drooping lower jaw, the downcast eye, the bent form, the slouching shoulders, the irresolute, halting, shambling gait—no purpose, no aim, no end in view—only to live on and endure life from day to day, and growl and grumble. Surely thought, or the lack of it, has been here an active agent in accomplishing sad results.

" I shall now become more or less visionary in my opinion and then stop. I believe that thoughts are things—intangible and invisible things, but none the less things—the finest and possibly the most powerful product of what we call ' matter.'

" For the sake of making an amusing theory I will assume that a person builds up a sort of thought structure all about them—an invisible envelope or garment of their ideas; that this thought envelope affects others coming near them, pleasantly or otherwise, according to its character; that the finer your organization the more sensitive your brain-threads, called nerves, the easier do you feel this thought coming from another, and this may account for your ' first impressions ' of people, which time so often verifies as correct. If you build up the ' I will ' structure, you draw the more will power to you and become the stronger continually. If you will even build up the ' I can't,' and ' it's no use trying,' and ' what's the use of living anyway?' garment, you drive off the will element and become the weaker and worse; you drive off eventually the people of will who might help you, but who are repelled by any one who is in a chronic state of ' flop.' "

A COLLOQUY BETWEEN LOCKE AND BAYLE.
[LORD LYTTLETON.]

LOCKE.—An enthusiast, who advanced doctrines prejudicial to society, or opposes any that are useful to it, has the strength of opinion. and the heat of a disturbed imagination to plead in alleviation of his fault. But your cool head and sound judgment can have no such excuse. I know very well there are passages in all your works, and those not few, where you talk like a rigid moralist. I have also heard that your character was irreproachable, good. But when, in the most labored parts of your writing, you sap the surest foundations of all moral duties, what avails it that in others, or in the conduct of your life, you appeared to respect them. How many, who have stronger passions than you had, and are desirous to get rid of the curb that restrains them, will lay hold of your scepticism to set themselves loose from all obligations of virtue. What a misfortune is it to have made such a use of such talents; it would have been better for you and for mankind, if you had been one of the dullest of Dutch theologians, or the most credulous monk in a Portuguese convent. The riches of the mind, like those of fortune, may be employed so perversely as to become a nuisance and pest, instead of an ornament and support to society.

BAYLE.—You are very severe upon me. But do you count it no merit, no service to mankind to deliver them from the frauds and fetters of priestcraft; from the deliriums of fanaticism, and from the terrors and follies of superstition. Consider how much mischief these have done in the world; even in the last age, what massacres; what civil wars; what convulsions of government; what confusion in society did they produce. Nay, in that we both lived in, though much more enlightened than the former. Did I not see them occasion a violent persecution in my own country; and can you blame me for striking at the root of these evils?

LOCKE.—The root of these evils, you well know, was false religion, but you struck at the true. Heaven and hell are not more different than the system of faith I defended, and that which produced the horrors of which you speak. Why would you so fallaciously confound them together in some of your writings that it requires much more judgment, and a more diligent attention than ordinary readers have, to separate them again, and to make the proper distinctions? This, indeed, is the great art of the most celebrated free-thinkers. They recommend themselves to warm and ingenuous minds, by lively strokes of wit, and by arguments really strong, against superstition, enthusiasm, and priestcraft. But, at the same time, they insidiously throw the colors of these upon the fair face of true religion, and dress her out in their garb, with a malignant intention to render her odious or despicable, to those who have not penetration enough to discover the impious fraud. Some of them may have thus deceived themselves, as well as others. Yet it is certain no book that ever was written by the most acute of these gentlemen is so repugnant to priestcraft, to spiritual tyranny, to all absurd superstitions, to all that can tend to disturb or injure society, as that gospel they so much affect to despise.

BAYLE.—Mankind are so made that, when they have been over-heated, they cannot be brought to a proper temper again till they have been over-cooled. My scepticism might be necessary to abate the fear and frenzy of false religion.

LOCKE.—A wise prescription, indeed, to bring on a paralytical state of the mind (for such a skepticism as yours is a palsy, which deprives the mind of all vigor and deadens its natural and vital powers) in order to take off a fever, which temperance and the milk of the evangelical doctrines would probably cure.

BAYLE.—I acknowledge that those medicines have a great power. But few doctors apply them untainted with the mixture of some harsher drugs, or some unsafe and ridiculous nostrums of their own.

LOCKE.—What you now say is too true. God has given us a most excellent physic for the soul in all its diseases; but bad and interested physicians, or ignorant and conceited quacks, adminis-ter it so ill to the rest of mankind that much of the benefit of it is unhappily lost.

ON THE IMMORTALITY OF THE SOUL.

[LORD BACON.]

I was yesterday walking alone, in one of my friend's woods, and lost myself in it very agreeably, as I was running over in mind the several arguments that established this great point, which is the basis of morality, and the source of all the pleasing hopes and secret joys that can arise in the heart of a reasonable creature.

I consider these several proofs drawn: First, from the nature of the soul itself, and particularly its innate vitality; which though not absolutely necessary to the eternity of its duration, has, I think, been evinced to almost a demonstration.

Secondly, from its passions and sentiments; as, particularly, from its love of existence; its horror of annihilation; and its hopes of immortality; with that secret satisfaction which it finds in the practice of virtue; and that uneasiness which follows upon the commission of vice.

Thirdly, from the nature of the Supreme Being, whose justice, goodness, wisdom, and veracity are all concerned in this point.

But among these and other excellent arguments for the immortality of the soul, there is one drawn from the perpetual progress of the soul to its perfection, without a possibility of ever arriving at it; which is a hint that I do not remember to have seen opened and improved by others, who have written on this subject, though it seems to me to carry a very great weight with it. How can it enter into the thoughts of man, that the soul, which is capable of immense perfections, and of receiving new improvements to all eternity, shall fall away into nothing almost as soon as it is created. Are such abilities made for no purpose? A brute arrives at a point of perfection that he can never pass; in a few years he has all the endowments he is capable of, and were he to live ten thousand years more, would be the same thing he is at present. Were a human soul thus at a stand in her accomplishments; were her faculties to be full blown, and incapable of farther enlargement: I could imagine she might fall away insensibly, and drop at once into a state of annihilation. But can we believe a thinking being that is in a perpetual progress of improvement, and traveling on from perfection, after having just looked abroad into the works of her Creator, and made a few discoveries of His infinite goodness, wisdom, and power, must perish at her first setting out, and in the very beginning of her inquiries. Man, considered only in his present state, seems sent into the world merely to propagate his kind. He provides himself with a successor, and immediately quits his post to make room for him. He does not seem born to enjoy life, but to deliver it down to others.

This is not surprising to consider in animals, which are formed for our use, and which can finish their business in a short life.

The silkworm after having spun her task lays her eggs and dies. But a man cannot take in his full measure of knowledge, has not time to subdue his passion, establish his soul in virtue, and come up to the perfection of his nature, before he is hurried off the stage.

Would an infinitely wise Being make such glorious creatures for so mean a purpose? Can he delight in the production of such abortive intelligence, such short-lived, reasonable beings? Would he give us talents that are not to be exerted? Capacities that are never to be gratified?

How can we find that wisdom which shines through all His

works in the formation of man without looking on this world as only a nursery for the next; and without believing that the several generations of rational creatures, which rise up and disappear in such quick succession, are only to receive their first rudiments of existence here, and afterwards to be transplanted into a more friendly climate, where they may spread and flourish to all eternity?

There is not, in my opinion, a more pleasing and triumphant consideration in religion, than this of the perpetual progress, which the soul makes towards the perfection of its nature, without ever arriving at a period in it. To look upon the soul as going on from strength to strength; to consider she is to shine forever with new accessions of glory, and brighten to all eternity; that she will be still adding virtue to virtue, and knowledge to knowledge; carries in it something wonderfully agreeable to that ambition which is natural to the mind of man. Nay, it must be a prospect pleasing to God himself, to see his creation for ever beautifying in His eyes; and drawing nearer to Him, by greater degrees of resemblance.

Methinks this single consideration, of the progress of a finite spirit to perfection, will be sufficient to extinguish all envy in inferior natures, and all contempt in superior. That cherub, which now appears as a god to a human soul, knows very well that the period will come about in eternity, when the human soul shall be as perfect as he himself now is; nay, when she shall look down upon that degree of perfection as much as she now falls short of it.

It is true, the higher nature still advances, and by that means preserves his distance and superiority in the scale of being; but he knows that, how high soever the station is of which he stands possessed at present, the inferior nature will, at length, mount up to it, and shine forth in the same degree of glory. With what astonishment and veneration may we look into our own souls, where there are such hidden stores of virtue and knowledge, such unexhausted sources of perfection! We know not yet what we shall be; nor will it ever enter into the heart of man to conceive the glory that will be always in reserve for him. The soul, considered with its Creator, is like one of those mathematical lines, that may draw nearer to another for all eternity, without a possibility of touching it; and can there be a thought so transporting, as to consider ourselves in these perpetual approaches to Him, who is the standard, not only of perfection, but happiness.

A FATHER'S PATHETIC APPEAL.

The following letter taken from the Covington "Commonwealth," was written by a father to a son of dissipated habits:

My Dear Son: What would you think of yourself if you should come to our bedside every night, and, waking us up, tell us you would not allow us to sleep any more?

This is what you are doing; and that is why I am up.

Your mother is nearly worn out with turning from side to side, and with sighing because you won't let her sleep.

That mother who nursed you in your infancy, toiled for you in childhood, and watched with pride and joy upon you as you were growing up to manhood, as she counted upon the comfort and support you would give her in her declining years. We read of the barbarous manner in which one of the Oriental nations punishes some of its criminals. It is by cutting the flesh slowly from the body in small pieces—slowly cutting off the limbs, beginning with the fingers and toes—until the wretched victim dies.

That is just what you are doing. You are killing your mother by inches.

You have planted many of the white hairs that have appeared in her head before their time. Your cruel hand is drawing the lines of sorrow on her dear face, making her look prematurely old. You might as well stick your knife in her, every time you come near her, for your conduct is stabbing her to the heart. You might as well bring her coffin and force her into it, for you are pressing her towards it with very rapid steps.

Would you tread on her body if prostrate on the floor? And yet with ungrateful steps you are treading on her heart and crushing out life and joy. No, I need not say joy, for that is a thing we have long ago ceased to see, because you have taken it away from us. Of course we have to meet many of our friends with smiles, but they little know the bitterness within.

You have taken the roses out of your sister's pathway and scattered thorns instead, and from the pain they inflict scalding tears are seen coursing down her cheeks. Thus you are blotting out her life as well as ours. And what can you promise yourself for the future?

Look at the miserable, bloated, ragged wretches whom you meet every day, and see in them an exact picture of what you are coming to and will be in a few years. Then in the end a drunkard's grave and a drunkard's doom! For the Bible says: "No drunkard shall inherit the kingdom." Where, then, will you be? If not in the Kingdom of God you must be somewhere else. Will not these considerations induce you to quit at once and for all time? And may God help you, for He can and will if you earnestly ask it.

Your affectionate but sorrow-stricken

FATHER.

THE OPIUM HABIT.

[MATHEWS.]

O, thou invisible spirit of opium, if thou hast no other name to be known by, let us call thee devil. (Shakespeare paraphrased.)—*Ed.*

It was in 1804, at the age of 19, that De Quincey first began taking opium to ease rheumatic pains in the face and head. This dangerous remedy having been recommended to him by a fellow student at Oxford, he entered a druggist's shop, and, like Thalaba in the witches' lair, wound about himself the first threads of a coil, which after the most gigantic efforts, he was never able wholly to shake off.

Using opium at first to quiet pain, he quickly found that it had mightier and more magical effects, and went on increasing the doses till in 1816 he was taking three hundred and twenty grains or eight thousand drops of laudanum a day. What a picture he has given us of the discovery he made! What a revelation the dark but subtle drug made to his spiritual eyes! What an agent of immortal and exalted pleasures! What an apocalypse of the world within him!

Here was a panacea for sorrow and suffering for the brain-ache and heart-ache—immunity from pain, and care, and all human woes. He swallowed a bit of the drug, and lo! the inner spirit's eyes were opened—a fairy ministrant had burst into wings, weaving a wondrous wand—a fresh tree of knowledge had yielded its fruit, and it seemed as good as it was beautiful. Happiness might now be bought for a penny and carried in the waistcoat pocket; portable ecstacies might now be had, corked up in a pint bottle, and peace of mind sent down in gallons by mail.

Here we may observe that De Quincey contradicts the statements which are usually made regarding opium. He denies that it intoxicates, and shows that there is such an insidiousness about it that it scarcely seems to be a qualification of the senses. The pleasure of wine is one that rises to a certain pitch, and then degenerates into a stupidity, while that of opium remains stationary for eight or ten hours.

Again, the influence of wine tends to disorder the mind, while opium tends to exalt the ideas, and yet to contribute to harmony and order in their arrangement. "The opium-eater feels that the diviner part of his nature is uppermost; that is, the moral affections are in a state of cloudless serenity, and over all is the great light of the majestic intellect." Alas! that this blissful state could not continue. But the very drug which had revealed to him such an abyss of divine enjoyment—which had given to him the keys of paradise, causing to pass before his spirit's eyes a never-ending succession of splendid imagery, the gorgeous coloring of sky and cloud, the pomp of woods and forests, the majesty of boundless oceans, and the grandeur of imperial cities, while to the ear, cleansed from their mortal infirmities, were borne the sublime anthem of the winds and waves, and a sevenfold chorus of halle-lujahs and harping symphonies—this very power became eventually its own avenging nenia, and inflicted torments compared with which those of Prometheus were as the bites of a gnat.

Of all the torments which opium inflicts upon its votary, perhaps there is no one more destructive of his peace than the sense of incapacity and feebleness—of inability to perform duties which conscience tells him he must not neglect. The opium-eater, De Quincey tells us, loses none of his moral sensibilities or aspirations: he wishes and longs as earnestly as ever to realize what he believes possible and feels to be exacted by duty; but the springs of his will are all broken, and his intellectual apprehension of what is possible infinitely outruns his power, not of execution only, but even of power to attempt.

He lies under the weight of incubus and nightmare; he lies in sight of all that he would fain perform; just a man forcibly confined to his bed by the mortal languor of a relaxing disease, who is compelled to witness injury or outrage offered to some object of his tenderest love. He curses the spells which chain him down from motion; he would lay down his life if he might but get up and walk; but he is as powerless as an infant, and cannot even attempt to rise. Of the cup of horrors which opium finally presents to its devotees De Quincey drank to the dregs, especially in his dreams at night, when the fearful and shadowy phantoms that flitted by his bedside made his sleep insufferable by the terror and anguish they occasioned.

Of these dreams, as portrayed in the "Confessions," and some of his other writings, we doubt if it would be possible to find a parallel in any literature, ancient or modern. Sometimes they are blended with appalling associations, encompassed with the power of darkness, or shrouded with the mysteries of death and the gloom of the grave. Now they are pervaded with unimaginable horrors of oriental imagery and mythological tortures; the dreamer is oppressed with tropical heat and vertical sunlight, and brings together all the physical prodigies of China and Hindostan.

He runs into pagodas, and is fixed for centuries at the summit, or in secret rooms; he flies from the wrath of Brahma through all the forests of Asia: Kishnu hates him; Seeba lays wait for him; he comes suddenly on Isis and Osiris: he has done a deed, they say, at which the Ibeis and the crocodile tremble; he is buried for a thousand years in stone coffins, with mummies and sphinxes, in narrow chambers at the heart of the eternal pyramids. He is kissed with cancerous kisses by crocodiles, and laid confounded with all unutterable, slimy things, amongst reeds and niletic mud.

Over every form, and threat, and punishment, and dim, sightless incarceration, brooded a sense of eternity and infinity that drove me into an oppression of madness. Into these dreams only, it was, with one or two slight exceptions, that any circumstances of physical horror entered. All before had been moral and spiritual terrors. But here the main agents were ugly birds, or snakes, or crocodiles, especially the last. The cursed crocodile became to me the object of more horrors than almost all the rest. I was compelled to live with him: and (as was always the case, almost in my dreams), for centuries.

I escaped sometimes, and found myself in Chinese houses, with cane tables, etc. All the feet of the tables, sofas, etc., soon became instinct with life; the abominable head of the crocodile, and his leering eyes, looked out at me, multiplied into a thousand repetitions; and I stood loathing and fascinated. And so often did this hideous reptile haunt my dreams, that many times the very same dream was broken up in the very same way. I heard gentle voices speaking to me (I hear everything when I am sleeping), and instantly I awoke; it was broad noon, and my children were standing, hand in hand, at my bedside; come to show me their colored shoes, or new frocks, or to let me see them dressed for going out. I protest that so awful was the transition from the damned crocodile, and the other unutterable monsters and abortions of my dreams, to the sight of innocent *human* nature and infancy, that in the mighty and sudden revulsion of mind, I wept, and could not forbear it, as I kissed their faces.

Anon, there would come suddenly a dream of a far different character—a tumultuous dream—commencing with music, and a multitudinous movement of infinite cavalcades filing off, and the tread of innumerable armies. The morning was come of a mighty day—a day of crisis and of ultimate hope for human nature, then suffering mysterious eclipse, and laboring in some dread extremity.

Somewhere, but I know not where—somehow, by some beings, I know not by whom—a battle, a strife, an agony was traveling through all its stages, was evolving itself like the catastrophe of some mighty drama, with which my sympathy was the more insupportable, from deepening confusion as to its local scene, its cause, its nature, and its undecipherable issue.

I (as is usual in dreams, where of necessity we make ourselves central to every movement), had the power, and yet had not the power, to decide it. I *had* the power, if I could raise myself to will it; and yet again had *not* the power, for the weight of twenty Atlantics was upon me, or the oppression of inexpiable guilt.

"Deeper than ever plummet," I lay inactive. Then like a chorus the passion deepened. Some greater interest was at stake, some mightier cause, than ever yet the sword had pleaded, or trumpet had proclaimed. Then came sudden alarms, hurryings to and fro, trepidations of innumerable fugitives—I know not whether from the good cause or the bad—darkness and light; tempest and human faces; and, at last, with the sense that all was lost, female forms, and the features that were worth all the world to me, and but a moment allowed, and clasped hands, with heart-breaking partings, and then everlasting farewells; and with a sigh such as the caves of hell sighed, when the incestuous mother uttered the abhored name of death, the sound was reverberated everlasing farewells! and again, and yet again reverberated everlasting farewells!

HORATIO SEYMOUR'S ADDRESS.

The following admirable address, delivered before the inmates in Auburn Prison, N. Y., will be read with great interest, as it contains such grand ideas as can only emanate from a great mind like Horatio Seymour's.—*Ed.*

ADDRESS.

I have declined all invitations this year to make public addresses, but when your Warden asked me to speak to you to-day I made up my mind to do so, although at the hazard of my health. My interest in the inmates of this and other prisons grows out of official duties, as I have had to act on many cases of applications for pardons. I have learned, from a long experience with men in all conditions of life, that none are without faults and none without virtues. I have studied characters with care. I have had to deal with Presidents and with prisoners. I have associated with those held in high honor by the American people. On the other hand, the laws of our State have placed the lives of criminal men in my hands, and it has been my duty to decide if they should live or die. The period in which I took the most active part in public affairs was one of great excitement, when passions and prejudices were aroused: and, in common with all others engaged in the controversies of the day, I have felt the bitterness of partisan strife; nevertheless, experience has taught me to think kindly of my fellow-men. The longer I live the better I think of their hearts and the less of their heads. Everywhere, from the President's mansion to the prisoner's cell, I have learned the wisdom of that prayer which begs that we may be delivered from temptation.

Another great truth is taught by experience: hope is the great reformer. We must instill this in men's minds if we wish to cultivate their virtues or enable them to overcome their vices. It has been said that despair is the unpardonable sin; for it paralyzes every sentiment that leads to virtue or happiness. To help us do our duty, we must cherish hope, which gives us courage and charity, which gives us hopes for others. For this reason, when Governor of this State, I did all I could to gain the passage of laws which enable each one of you, by good conduct, to shorten the term of your imprisonment; and if I had my way, you would have a share in the profits of your labor. But I stand before you to-day to speak of another ground of hope, of a higher and more lasting character than mere gain or shortened terms of punishment; and what I have to say does not point to you alone, but to men of all conditions. I do not mean to take the place of those who teach you your religious duties. They are far more able than I am to make these clear to your minds; yet it is sometimes the case that we see things in lights in which they are not usually placed before us, and some thoughts which have occurred to me, in a review of my life, may be of interest and value to you. When we grow old, we are struck with the fleetness of time; our lives seem to be compassed into one brief period; we suddenly find that pursuits we have followed are closed, and we are confronted with the question, not what we have gained, nor what positions we have held, but what we are in ourselves. We know it is our duty to do what is right, and to avoid doing wrong, but when we look back, if we add up all of our good deeds on the one hand, and our bad acts on the other, we find a startling balance against us. When men reach my time of life, their minds turn toward the past, and they travel backward the paths they have followed. They see things from the opposite side from which they were viewed in youth onward, and are struck by truths which never break upon their minds until they look back upon them.

Sitting before my fire on a winter evening, and musing, as old men are apt to do, about their acts, their errors, their successes, or their failures, it occurred to me what I would do if I had the power, and was compelled to wipe out twenty acts of my life. At first it seemed as if this was an easy thing to do. I had done more than twenty wrong things for which I had always felt regret, and was about to seize my imaginary sponge and rub them out at once, but I thought it best to move with care, to do as I had done to others, lay my character out upon the dissecting table and trace all influences which had made or marred it. I found, to my surprise, if there were any golden threads running through it, they were wrought out by the regrets felt at wrongs; that these regrets had run through the course of my life, guiding my footsteps through all its intricacies and problems; and if I should obliterate all of these acts, to which these golden threads were attached, whose lengthening lines were woven into my very nature, I should destroy what little there was of virtue in my moral make-up. Then I learned that the wrong act, followed by the just regret, and by thoughtful caution to avoid like errors, made me a better man than I should have been if I had never fallen. In this, I found hope for myself and hope for others, and I tell you who sit before me, as I say to all in every condition, that if you will you can make yourselves better men than if you had never fallen into errors or crimes. A man's destiny does not turn upon the fact of his doing or not doing wrong—for all men will do it—but of how he bears himself, what he does and what he thinks, after the wrong act. It was well said by Confucius, that a man's character is decided, not by the number of times he falls, but by the number of times he lifts himself up. I do not know why evil is permitted in this world, but I do know that each one of us has the magical power to transmute it into good. Every one before me can, if he will, make his past errors sources of moral elevation. Is this not a grand thought, which should not only give us hope, but which should inspire us with firm purposes to exercise this power which makes us akin to the Almighty; for He has given it to us and has pointed out in His words how we shall use it. The problem meets us at every step. There is nothing we do which will not make us better or worse. I do not speak merely of great events, but of the thoughts upon our beds, the toil in the workshop, and the little duties which attend every hour. God, in His goodness, does not judge us so much by what we do; but when we have done things, right or wrong, our destiny mainly turns upon what we think and do after their occurrence. It is then we decide if they shall lift us up to a higher level, or bear us down to a lower grade of morals. Our acts mainly spring from impulses or accidents—the sudden temptation, imperfect knowledge, or erring judgment. It is the afterthought that gives them their hue. The world may not see this: it may frown upon the deed and upon the man, who, nevertheless, by his regrets, makes it one which shall minister to purity and virtue in all his after-life. You, who sit before me, in some ways have advantages over other men whose minds are agitated by the hopes and fears of active pursuits, who find no time for thoughts which tend to virtue and to happiness. With each of you, in a little time, the great question will be—not if you are to be set free, not what the world thinks of you, not what you have— but what you are; for death often knocks at the door of your cells, and some of your number are carried from their narrow walls to the more narrow walls of the grave.

Let it not be thought that I prove wrong may be done so that good may follow. With Saint Paul, I protest against such inference from the truth that men are saved by repentance of their sins.

But let us look further into this subject, for it deeply concerns us. Though we are unable to recall the errors of the past, we may so deal with them that they may promote our virtue, our wisdom, and happiness. Upon this point I am not theorizing. Whoever thinks, will learn that human experience proves this. Let us take the case of our errors. We should find, if we could rub them all out, that we should destroy the wisdom they have given us, if we have taken care to make our errors teach us wisdom. Who could spare their sorrows? How much that is kind and sympathetic in our natures, which leads us to minister to the griefs of others, and thus to gain consolations for ourselves, grow out of what are felt as keen calamities when they befall us.

Following out the line of my thoughts, when I assumed that I had the power and was compelled to drown in Lethean waters certain acts, I found I could not spare errors which call forth regrets, mistakes which teach us wisdom, or the sorrows which soften character and make us sensible of the sympathies which give beauty to the intercourse of life. As I had to obliterate twenty events, I found I could best spare the successes or triumphs which had only served to impart courage in the battle of life and had but little influence in forming character. It is true, that wherever and whatever we are, we can so deal with the past, that we can make it give up to us virtue and wisdom. We can, by our regrets, do more than the alchemist aims at when he seeks to transmute base metals into gold, for we can make wrong the seed of right and righteousness; we can transmute error into wisdom; we can make sorrow bloom into a thousand forms like fragrant flowers. These great truths should not only give us contentment with our positions, but hope for the future. The great question, what are we, presses itself upon us as we grow old, or flashes upon us when our lives are cut short by accident or disease. Within these walls, but few days pass without that question being forced upon the minds of some who have reached the end of life's journey. Surely, it should give hope and consolation to all to feel that they can, in the solitude of the cell, or in the gloom of the prison, by thought, by self-examination, make the past, with its crimes, its errors, and its sorrows, the very means by which they can lift themselves into higher and happier conditions. This work of transmuting evil into good, is a duty to be done by all conditions of men, and it can be wrought out as well in the prisoner's cell, as in the highest and most honorable position, for when you do this, you work by the side of the Almighty. All human experience accords with the higher teachings of religion, that holds out hope to men who feel regret for every evil act. I wish to call your minds to that amazing truth, that there is a Being who rules the world with such benevolence, that He enables weak and erring mortals, if they will, to turn their very sorrows and errors into sources of happiness.

We have many theories in these days in which men try to tell us how the world, acting upon certain fixed laws, has made itself; that it goes on by a progress that regards nothing but certain rules of advancement, regardless of all other considerations save their own irresistible self-compelling principles. But here we have a truth not only given us in Holy Writ, but proved by our experience, that mental regret will convert a material wrong into a blessing, or, if the offender wills it, will make the same a hundredfold more hurtful if he rejoices in his wrong-doing, or hardens his heart against regret. Materialism, evolution, pantheism, or any of the theories which deny the government of an intelligent God, are all phases of fatalism, and are confuted by this truth, that we can, by conforming to His laws, which demand repentance, convert evil into good, or by violating them make evil tenfold more deadly and destructive. We can, by our own minds and sentiments, change the influence of material events, and vary the action of laws which govern the world. If man, with all his weakness, can do this, it can only be by the aid of a higher power which shapes, directs, and regulates.

I know that what I have said is but an imperfect statement of great truths, compared with the teachings of the pulpit which you hear every Sunday. As my purpose is merely to speak to you of what I have learned in the walks of life, I can give you from this narrow field but partial views of great truths. They may be of no value to you, yet I trust you will accept them at least as proof of my sympathies with your condition and sorrows, for if any ambition lingers in the breast of him who speaks to you now, it is that he may be the friend and adviser of the erring and wrong-doer. He has been taught by self-examination and the study of others, that we all belong to that class, and that we owe to one another any aid we can give to our fellows when they fall by the wayside.

BE CAREFUL WHAT YOU SAY.

In speaking of a person's faults,
  Pray don't forget your own;
Remember those with homes of glass,
  Should seldom throw a stone;
If we have nothing else to do
  But talk of those who sin,
'Tis better we commence at home,
  And from that point begin.

We have no right to judge a man,
  Until he's fairly tried;
Should we not like his company,
  We know the world is wide.
Some may have faults—and who has not?—
  The old as well as young;
Perhaps we may, for aught we know,
  Have fifty to their one.

I'll tell you of a better plan,
  And find it works full well;
To try my own defects to cure
  Before of others' tell;
And though I sometimes hope to be
  No worse than some I know,
My own shortcomings bid me let
  The faults of others go.

Then let us all, when we commence
  To slander friend or foe.
Think of the harm one word would do
  To those we little know.
Remember curses, sometimes, like
  Our chickens, "roost at home;"
Don't speak of others' faults until
  We have none of our own.

THE PRISON BELL.*

It was night, and in my lonely cell,
The pale moon's playful shadows fell
So bright, I dreamt that all on earth
Was changed once more to smiles and mirth.

The morning dawned, the rising sun
His glorious course through heaven begun,
When honest man, with heartfelt strides,
Goes whistling by the prison sides.

While I, in bonds, with heart downcast,
Deep grieving present and the past,
Lay half unconscious in my cell,
'Till summoned by the prison bell.

Day passed; and when all days are passed,
And I on death's waves am cast,
May I a pitying Savior see,
To let this captive prisoner free!
To see the joys that heart can't tell,
To hear no more the prison bell.

* DEAR BROTHERS: This was written by one who was a thief for forty-six
years, and was a prisoner thirty-five years in eleven different prisons, but who
has found out, by the grace of God, through the blood of Christ, that honest
labor has its reward.

IN PRISON.

God pity the wretched prisoner,
  In his lonely cell to-day,
Whatever the sin that tripped him,
  God pity him still I pray.
Only a glimpse of sunshine,
  Through the walls of stone,
Only a patch of azure
  To starve his hopes upon:
Only surging memories
  Of a past that is better gone;
Only scorn from woman,
  Only hate from men:
Only remorse to whisper
  Of a life that might have been!
Once we were little children,
  And then our unstained feet
Were led by a gentle mother,
  Towards the golden street.
Therefore if in life's forest
  We since have lost our way,
For the sake of her who loved us,
  God pity us still I pray.
O Mother, gone to heaven!
  With earnest prayer I ask
That your eye may not look earthward
  On the failure of your task!
For even in those mansions,
  The choking tears would rise,
Though the fairest hand in heaven
  Should wipe them from your eyes.
And you who judge us harshly—
  Are you sure the stumbling stone,
That tripped the feet of others,
  Might not have bruised your own?

Are you sure the sad-faced angel
  Who writes our errors down,
Will ascribe to you more honor,
  Than him on whom you frown?
Or if a steadier purpose
  Unto your life be given,
A stronger will to conquer,
  A smoother path to heaven—
If when temptations meet you,
  You crush them with a smile,
If you can chain pale Passion,
  And keep your lips from guile—
Then bless the hand that crowned you!
  Remembering as you go,
It was not your own endeavor
  That shaped your nature so;
And sneer not at the weakness
  Which made a brother fail,
For the hand that lifts the fallen.
  God loves the best of all.